THE
CHRISTMAS
COTTAGE

MAELYN BJORK

BookSide Press
877-741-8091
www.booksidepress.com
orders@booksidepress.com

PROLOGUE

Jenna Barlow heard a soft knock at her attic room door. After she wiped away her tears, she hurried to open it.

"Sister Jenna, come, come. We must measure you, so that we can hem your wedding dress. Follow me down stairs." Sister wife, Erma said. Dutifully, Jenna walked to the large country kitchen of the Barlow household.

"Now step out of your dress and let us help you into the gown we picked for your wedding." Erma commanded.

The young girl crossed her arms and held tightly to the dress she wore. "Can't I take it up to my room to try on?" There was a plea in her voice.

"No, don't be silly. We all wear the same underwear. It's nothing we haven't seen before. You know we sewed them for you. Now, Sister Wife, Rebecca, help me put this dress over her head." The dress floated down over Jenna, and Rebecca fastened the zipper.

"My, she's a tiny one. We'll have to tighten up the sash and seam in the sides. Now Jenna, stand on the stool."

Jenna obeyed,

"Stand still girl. We will move around you. It will be faster for us to do that." Quickly they pinned the hem and marked it.

Once the dress was measured, the two sister wives helped her out of it and handed her the dress she had been wearing. "Now go upstairs and take a good shower and wash your hair. When you go to his room tonight, Elder Richards will want to take down your hair. That will be after the wedding of course." Erma giggled.

"When we're finished, we'll bring the dress up to you. Now pack your things in this backpack. Once you're married to him, you'll become the youngest wife in his household, and his other wives will see to your needs."

Jenna nodded and scurried to her room and then to the bathroom in the hall. She had another crying spell in the shower, slowly toweling off and drying her waist length blond hair.

The day seemed to crawl by, and yet too soon the two women came with her dress, white flat heeled shoes, and a veil. The wedding was to take place in the chapel of the FLDS church building, in the town of River Mesa. After the ceremony there would to be a supper, and everyone in the town was invited to come eat, dance and enjoy the festivities.

Jenna was driven to the building and escorted to a small room next to the women's restroom. In there was a full-length mirror, and she finally could examine this dress she wore. It had been designed for another teenage bride in the town. It was of a textured taffeta, with a full skirt, long, leg-o-muffin sleeves, and a high neckline. The veil was short, made of tulle, and sewn to wide velvet band. She stared at her reflection and again began to cry. *It's only been three weeks since my mother died. They promised that I wouldn't have to marry Eldon Richards for a few months. He's forty-nine years old. Only three years younger than my father. I'm only fifteen, and I don't want to marry anyone. Please God if you can hear me. Help Me.*

Though the actual ceremony took only a few minutes, to a sad and terrified Jenna, it seemed to fly by in a blur. Her new husband gave her a chaste kiss. *Eu! he has bad breath.* He then led to her place at the head table. A plate of food was set before her, but her stomach roiled and she could not eat anything. Somewhat later Arden her new husband, gray haired, bad breath and all, took her by the hand and led her to the dance floor. While the guests applauded, they danced for a few minutes. Suddenly, two of the other elders of the church came up to Elder Richards and spoke softly to him.

"I must see to a situation." He said, and led Jenna back to her place at the table. As she slid into the chair, she had a sudden thought, an idea. *No one really knows what he said to me. Maybe I can escape.* "Excuse me, I must go home for my things." She said to the other people at the table. She hurried out of the church building and ran to her home and up to her old attic room. She was winded and had to catch her breath, but quickly she changed from the wedding attire to her oldest dress and tennis shoes. She grabbed her backpack and moved as quietly as she could out of the house and ran for the highway. She walked north close along the side of the road, trying to stay near trees and tall brush.

Traffic whizzed by seeming not to see her. She wasn't sure how long she walked, but soon grew weary from the emotional day she had endured, and not eating much. Behind her a vehicle slowed, and she jumped off the road to the side and hunkered down. The dark colored SUV slowed to a stop and the passenger side window rolled down."Do you need a ride, girl?" A feminine voice called out.

Jenna stood up not knowing what to do. Then her attention turned to a car turning out on the highway from a road half a mile or so behind. It could be people from River Mesa searching for her. She glanced at the woman who had called to her. She wasn't a real young woman and had a nice profile. "Yes, I could use a ride to St. George." She walked to the rear door and climbed in.

The woman accelerated the car and said. "Duck down. The car behind me is driving very close to the side of the road. I think they are searching for someone. I'm Brenda Thompson. Did you see one of the flyers I scattered along the road?"

"Yes, a few months ago, but I forgot about it until tonight. My name is Jenna." She fastened her seatbelt and settled back against the seat, and brushed the soft upholstery with her hand. She took a deep breath and released it. "This is a nice car. What kind is it?"

Brenda laughed. "A Dodge. Do you like cars?"

"Yes." She was so relived to be away from Elder Richards, his household and especially his hands that felt rough and sent chills through her when he touched her. For awhile Jenna watched the road flying by the window, but then she relaxed and soon fell asleep. She was roused by a change in the sound of the car's engine, and they slowed turning down a street with several houses on both sides.

The woman drove the car into a garage, and she came around to where Jenna was sitting. "Come in Jenna."

She followed the woman taken into a kitchen. Then the she led Jenna upstairs to bedroom with two sets of bunk beds in it. Two of the beds were occupied by girls. "This one is for you. She patted an empty bottom bed. "The bathroom is right across the hall. I'll find some clothes for you in the morning, and we'll talk. Good night." She smiled and patted Jenna on her shoulder and went downstairs.

Jenna lay in the bed and stared at the frame of the bed above. She felt as if a great burden had been lifted off her young shoulders. It was almost happiness she felt to be away from Elder Richards and the wedding night that would have happened. Somehow, she managed to sleep.

The next morning a pair of jeans, a tee shirt and some normal, feminine underwear lay across the bottom of her bed. One of the girls came into the room and sat on the opposite bunk.

"Hi, I'm Fern. Do you remember me, because I think I remember you?" Jenna could see a freckle faced, red headed girl smiling at her.

"Are you from River Mesa? Did you run away, too?" Jenna sat up and studied her roommate.

"Yes, about eight months ago. You were so smart and brave to do what you did. You won't be sorry. Get dressed, Brenda is making pancakes."

Later after breakfast, Brenda and Jenna sat at the table and talked. "I know this is all new to you, but the reason I picked you up is to allow you the chance, and really understand, and see how normal teenage girls live. I want help you get the education you deserve, so that you will be able to make your own decisions. When we grow stronger, we can find ways to help other people. Especially when they are in a situation when you are able rescue them. Someday perhaps, you may have the chance to help someone running from something bad, and you'll be given an opportunity to save them, too."

Thus began the first day of Jenna's new life.

CHAPTER ONE

Fifteen years later

Jenna Barlow stifled a yawn, pushed up the sleeve of her gray, wool blazer, and glanced at her watch. Eight- fifty P.M. She sighed. The meeting of the Alta-Angeles Corporation had been in full swing since six- thirty P.M. that evening.

Percy Roberts finally turned to the CEO of the advertising agency. "That about sums it up for the year. I thank all of you for your patience on this Eve of Christmas Eve." He laughed self-consciously.

The *boss*, Walter Richter of the agency, stood. "We'll see all of you back here on December 27th. We welcome Jenna Barlow, our newest member to the Salt Lake City offices. She will give us a presentation of our new account, *Wilderness Adventures, Inc.*

One by one the people seated around the table picked up their belongings and exited to the cloak room. One of the secretaries went to the window and raised the blinds. "It's snowed several inches out there while we've been sitting here. Everyone be careful driving or walking to your destinations."

Great. Jenna thought. She had been forced to park on the roof of the building, because it shared the parking garage with the largest shopping mall in Salt Lake City. The garage had been filled to capacity with last minute shoppers' cars. She trudged off the elevator and into a heavy snow storm.

By the time she had stowed her laptop, and changed from dress shoes to snow boots, it took her several minutes to clean the snow from the car's windows. Her head and shoulders were covered with a heavy dusting of snow, so she used the window brush clean off her coat. Finally, she began the descent from the roof to the streets below, eight stories down. Going from floor to floor meant taking a curving tube to the next level. Then she needed to drive across that level to the next descending curved tube; Which allowed other cars on that floor to get in line. All vehicles must cross the garage to reach the next curve and on down to the street.

As she crossed level four, she heard a pop, pop. *Gun Shots?* To her right she caught a blur of movement. Her passenger door flew open and a man jumped in. *Damn, I forgot to lock the car doors.*

"Keep driving, just leave here. Please!"

At first, all she noticed was that the man was tall, and wore a leather jacket. "Get out of my car!" Jenna screamed. She slammed on the brakes and pushed at his shoulder. Her car fishtailed, and she had to touch the gas pedal to straighten it out. She heard a groan from her unwelcome passenger. When she pulled her hand away from him, it was covered with blood.

"Who are you?" She yelled, but was forced to focus. She must enter the next curve to level four. Before the man could answer, she watched her driver's side mirror explode. "What? Damn it! Who's shooting? Is it because you're in my car?!" She took the curve and straightened out to the floor four. She noticed another car right behind her, a black Mercedes. She accelerated, allowing a large, older minivan to slide in between her car and the Mercedes.

"Who's chasing you and now me? Augh! I hope we get out of here alive and in one piece." At level two she shot out through the exit of the garage and turned east. "Now explain yourself. Who are you, and now I'd better find some police."

"I believe I have something that they want." He glanced at her. "It's my shoulder." He touched his left shoulder. She was surprised. He spoke with a British accent?

"I'm driving us out of the downtown area as quickly as possible, and taking you to a police station or a doctor. Hey, watch it. This is a new car. I don't want blood on the leather seats."

"Oh, sorry." He took in a ragged breath. "My medical identification, along with my passport, are in my hotel room, I cannot go to a medical facility in the States."

She glanced at the floor and saw a briefcase between his legs. "Don't you even have a driver's license? Where are you staying? They could probably help you. Which hotel?"

"I've a room at the Sheraton. But I don't know- - - - - - -?" He took a big breath and it came out a groan.

She took a right turn and drove a block south toward the hotel. Then she glanced out her rear-view mirror. "Never mind, the Mercedes is right behind us. We won't be able to stop here. I'll need to find hospital or clinic somewhere else.. Your shoulder has been wounded, right?"

Jenna's focus went to the windshield wipers as they moved at a steady beat. Now the car began warming up inside. She found that the car handled well in this heavy snowfall. It was quite new, and she had only owned it a short while.

"You're perceptive lass. Yes, my left shoulder." He dragged in another breath. "Sorry, I don't know your name. I'm Alistair Powell, and I'm afraid right now, I'm _not_ at your service." He tried for a laugh, but it came out as another groan.

"I'm Jenna Barlow. Now what are you doing in Salt Lake City?" She took another left and drove to Fourth South Street. Shooting through a yellow light, she slid into the parking lot of the Sheraton, but the Mercedes was right on her tail. She swung out of the lot and took another left and drove east.

This street led up to the campus of the University of Utah. Now it was dark and quiet because of the Christmas Holidays. She drove east up past the University. Or at least this was what she remembered. She had not lived in Salt Lake for over ten years.

"You still haven't told me why you're in Salt Lake." Jenna asked through gritted teeth.

"I came here for a simple demonstration of a product my company may want to purchase." He coughed and a moan slipped out.

"Okay, - - - - - . Just so you know we're passing the University of

Utah complex to the left. I think there's a hospital up there. Now I just have to find the right exit." She glanced out her driver's side mirror, and spotted the Mercedes a half a block behind. She accelerated and watched the hospital exit go by. "Damn, I missed the exit. I just moved here myself, and I'm not too sure if I can remember the streets around here." She mumbled.

She motored through a red light, but could see the Mercedes was forced to stop at the light. "Hey, they haven't given up. Where is a cop when you *need* one?" She felt her neck muscles tighten, and tension between her shoulders. Some of it was stress, but strangely, she also felt a thrill of the chase, or being chased. *Jenna this isn't a TV show.* Yet she had watched many movies and TV shows having scenes like this. Now she was living it. *Hey, stay focused girl. You've spent too many evenings home alone.*

The snow continued, seemingly to be in sheets of white falling straight down from the gray clouds. Visibility was poor, but there was less wind. At this higher elevation, the roadway was becoming slippery.

"Now why are these people after you? You said you have something that they want. What is it, the plans for a new bomb?"

"I am not acquainted with these individuals personally, but I am with their methods." Alistair said.

"Are they locals, or imported thugs?" Jenna focused and was careful to drive at the safest possible speed. She knew a spin out would cause them to lose more time, than picking up speed and maybe get both of them shot. "I think there's a hospital at Thirty-ninth South and about Eleventh East. I can take you there."

"What was your original destination? Do you have many miles to go?" He asked.

"We'll worry about that later." She took Thirty-third South Street down the hill and turned-on Thirty-ninth south and Eleventh east. Through the blinding snow she could see the outline of the large building. That had to be the hospital. "Okay for the moment we've lost them. I'm going to pull up to the emergency entrance. Can you manage to walk into the building alone?"

"Yes, but- - - - -." He turned to her. "Please don't leave me."

"No hesitating. Just get in there. I'll park the car and follow you in."

Awkwardly he eased out of the car and walked in through the double doors of the emergency area. She drove around the corner and headed for the street exit. *When they see his gunshot wound, he'll be okay without me, damn, there's the Mercedes!* She drove around to the east side of the hospital and to another entrance close to the emergency area. She jumped from the car locking it with the remote and ran into the corridor that led to the emergency area. Just as she entered, a doctor stood with a clipboard in his hand. Otherwise, the waiting room was empty.

"Are you Alistair's cousin, Ms. Barlow?" He asked.. "I've called the Cottonwood Police. We're waiting for radiology to come and get Alistair. They'll want a statement."

"Where is he?" She asked, and tried not to sound too anxious.

"Room E-3." He gestured through the door.

He turned around and she followed him into the emergency treatment area, but he kept going toward a group of medical people. She could hear laughter, and the clink of glasses. She ducked into E-3 "Come on Alistair, we've got to get out of here." She threw his leather jacket at him.

"But shouldn't we- - - -."

"No, the thugs are here. She dragged him into the waiting area. "Stop!" She glanced out the tall window nest to the door. "Crap, the guy's carrying a gun." She studied the thug momentarily. *He looks Asian.* "We'll go out the east entrance." She grabbed the wounded man and hustled down the corridor, out the door and to her car. She opened the passenger door and shoved Alistair in. She had the car in gear and roared out of the east exit, drove half a block and turned east on Thirty-ninth South Street. As fast as she dared, she drove up the street which turned into a hill a few blocks farther later. She glanced over at Alistair. His head was lolling back against the seat.

"What did the doctor say about your wound? Oh, here come the police." She said.

"He said- - - - it was, ah- - - - - -, through and through. Sorry, he gave me- - - - -an inject- - - -." Alistair stopped talking and his head dropped to one side.

"Well, he's out. Let's just get away as fast as possible. She glanced into her rear-view mirror. "Ugh, the Mercedes. *When I get to the freeway, they won't catch me there. You're losing it Jenna, you're talking to yourself.*

Chapter Two

A heavily dressed policeman stomped into the hospital and asked for Alistair Powell, and his cousin Jenna. A medical tech escorted him to Room E.3 "They were here a few minutes ago. Let me check the radiology sheet." She glanced at the sheet hooked to the gurney. "Sorry, they must have left."

A growl of frustration. "Yeah, thanks anyway." The officer stomped back to his partner sitting in the black and white police truck.

"A silver or white Lexus went out and up Thirty-ninth with a black Mercedes right on her tail. Could be that some characters really _are_ chasing them." He spun the truck out and followed the other two vehicles east.

"It looks like the Lexus is having a better time negotiating the hill than the Mercedes."

"Can you get a look at the license plate on the Mercedes?" The officer said to his partner.

The officer in the passenger seat picked up some field glasses and studied the car two blocks ahead. "The storm isn't helping, maybe when we get to the top of the hill, I can- - - - - - -."

"The light's turning red. She'll have to stop. The Mercedes is right behind her." _pop,_ "Did you hear that? Those guys just took a shot at her. They _are_ up to foul play. Let's get 'em."

Jenna was forced to stop for a red light, and the Mercedes came right up behind them. Through the falling snow, Jenna thought she could see a police truck, close behind the Mercedes. The light turned green, and Jenna took a left. Another shot came from the Mercedes, and slammed into the edge of the rear hatch of her new Lexus. She flinched as she heard the bullet hit her car, but had to continue down the on-ramp turning north which would connect to I-80 East. She made the turn, and gunned the midsized car onto the Park City Lane. "I hope my car insurance covers bullet hole damage." She screamed.

Glancing through her rear-view mirror, she grinned in satisfaction. The Mercedes had taken the turn too fast, and slid cross- wise into a snow bank. The Black and White was right behind it.

She kept going and took the exit to Park City. *I suppose I may as well continue with the original plan, and go on to the retreat.* She glanced at the green glow of the dashboard clock. *It's already past eleven. I thought I'd be there by now. But with this massive snow storm, and a chase all through the eastside of Salt Lake County, all this craziness has slowed me down. Wounded passenger or not, I'll feel safer if I can get us there.*

Jenna continued to drive up Parley's Canyon. The snowy packed road and the blinding snow fall took all of the driving skill Jenna possessed. She had always like cars, and studied them. To her this Lexus was the best of all- wheel drive vehicles and equipped with over-sized all weather tires. This car would get them to her destination. At least she prayed it would.

*****

"Where are we going?" Jenna's passenger slowly asked.

"I decided the best thing to do was to continue on with my original plan and to go to a retreat for the weekend. It's in a rather secluded spot, but I hadn't planned on this weather." She chewed on her bottom lip. "However, this car will make it if anything can. So, relax. Are you in much pain?"

He shifted carefully under the seat belt. "Surprisingly, not. The injection he-- gave--- me must--- be working." His head dropped back on the seat and he closed his eyes.

"Good, no more stops, because I'm not sure if this storm is going to intensify or just blow itself out. I'm glad we at least got you into see a doctor, but now the Cottonwood Police will want to talk to us." She flashed him a look.

"Are there any signs of our pursuers?" He mumbled and coughed again. His breathing was slower. He coughed, cleared his throat, and stopped talking.

She continued to drive with caution, took I-80 east, and drove on through the night.

A few minutes later he sniffed, and struggled to sit up. "Are we still motoring to your retreat? No sign of the thugs?"

"No, I think we lost them. They went sideways in a snow bank at the freeway entrance, and I saw the black and white right behind them.

"Black and white, of what are you speaking?"

"A local police truck." She managed a tiny laugh. "They're all painted black and white."

"Do you think the authorities detained them? That would be in our favor." He nodded. "I can hang on, much more comfortable than I was earlier."

"We're doing okay. If we can make it over the summit without sliding off the road, I believe we will reach our destination."

"And our destination is?"

"We take the Coleville exit, and drive through a town called Coleville. On the outskirts is a retreat called Coleville Cliffs Resort."

"Is it a ski resort? I'd planned on visiting one of your ski areas while I was in America."

"Not for alpine skiing, but more for snow mobile riders." She had to stop talking and focus on her driving. The visibility had become, just what she could see a few feet ahead. All her focus went to guiding her Lexus on through this level five blizzard.

"Could you reach behind the seat and find a brown sack?" Jenna asked. There are some sodas in it. If possible, could you fetch me one? Have one yourself. You most likely need the extra fluid."

"Why do you want cold soda on a night like this?' He asked.

"It's for the caffeine, not the chill. I need to be alert." She put her hand out as he thrust a can into it. "Open it, if you're able." *Keep him busy, thinking about something else rather than his shoulder.*

He put the can between his knees, and with his right hand popped it open. He handed it to her, and used his cold soda to rub against his wounded shoulder.

Alistair dozed, but as the car slowed to a crawl he awoke. "Are we stuck?"

"No, I'm following in the tire tracks of a semi, and he's slowed to about fifteen miles an hour."

He glanced out the passenger side window. The visibility allowed him to see only to the shoulder of the road. He watched as a car slid off against the side. Another vehicle was facing out with the rear end off the pavement. Its headlights still illuminating the steady snowfall. In all of his 36 years of living, he had never seen a storm like this one.

Yet this young woman, Jenna, seemed cool, focused and in control of this automobile, and also their lives. They passed another car sliding down into an embankment on the opposite side. They continued the slow climb, but the sound of the engine changed. They had reached the summit, and it seemed it was all downhill now.

*****

Jenna sighed audibly. "Whew, we made it to the summit. Now we go down, and down." The truck's speed increased, but for the next few miles, Jenna stay behind him.. Alistair watched as they passed the sign for the Park City exit. "I thought about taking you to Park City, but decided that if the thugs followed us later it would be easier to find us there. Besides I'm not that familiar with Park City, and I don't know where the hospital is."

The road narrowed to two lanes, and Jenna passed the truck, and honked at the driver. He honked back. As the road turned more to the north, the storm became lighter. "How did you decide to follow the Lorry?" He asked.

"Lorry? Oh, the semi-truck and trailer. I learned to do that while driving to Colorado one October. My friend, Fern and I drove through mountain passes of over twelve thousand feet elevation, and found ourselves driving into the first snow storm of the season. The car we were driving was nothing like this one and had no snow tires. So, Fern decided to follow the semi through a mountain pass. We managed to keep going, when other cars got stuck, or had to turn back."

"Why were you two girls driving to Colorado?"

"We shared a room, and Fern had met this young man, and she thought she was in love with him. He was stationed at Camp Carson near Colorado Springs. So, we took a weekend to go visit him."

"Were they in love?" He asked.

"Yes, but they couldn't marry at that time, because he was being sent to Iraq. After he did two tours in that *lovely* country, he came back to St. George and then they married. It was the first marriage of a girl in the group home."

"You lived in a group home? Why were you there?"

"Perhaps I'll tell you all the gritty details of my past some other time."

Alistair blinked his eyes closed. Despite the stiffness in his shoulder, the pain was much less. He couldn't seem to keep his eyes open. He was exhausted. As he tried to relax, he wondered how a simple meeting with a fledging tech company had to put him in harm's way. Why were thugs, as Jenna called them, trying to kill him for possessing a disc?

After being chased, shot and wounded in a parking garage, he now was being transported by a pretty blonde girl he had just barely met, through a level four blizzard, to an undisclosed destination in rural Utah. He thought of home, of Christmases in York. He had planned to ring up his parents on the Eve of Christmas. They would be amazed that he could call from nine thousand miles away, from a western state called Utah. Where was his cellular telephone? He didn't have the energy to search his briefcase for it.

Jenna glanced at the man in the front seat next to her. His head lolled against the back of the leather bucket seat. *Now, instead of being alone, I have a Brit for a passenger, interesting. Why was he in Salt Lake at Christmas Time? What knowledge or item did he possess that others wanted enough to kill him for it? And why had she continued to rescue him, rather than leave him at the hospital? Deep down she knew. When she had run away, been alone and frightened there was a kind woman who rescued her. A wonderful woman who had helped her to adjust to a new life. She supposed it was Karma.*

Soon though, she would need to learn all his secrets. Right now, she must watch for the exit to Coleville. There, the sign read. COLEVILLE EXIT ONE MILE. She watched carefully and took the next exit which became a frontage road.

She passed a Chevron Station. The street sign now read Fifth West. Traveling along this street she drove by a restaurant, the post office, and a shop called Sally's Quilts and Crafts. All of them dark and shuttered. She turned east and the road became residential, with various houses on fairly large tracks of land. The further she drove the larger the empty land became between houses and sometimes a barn. Soon it was country. Just snow-covered fields. The storm had turned into flurries, but there was over half a foot on the ground, and the road had not been cleared that evening.

Finally, she reached the gate of the resort she sought: Coleville Cliffs Resort. She stopped and reached for her purse. Pulling out a key card she pushed it into the slot, marked ENTRANCE. The gate struggled to swing open, barely cutting through the snow.

For a moment her car was hung up on the new snow, but she put it in reverse, then dropped it into low gear and gunned the car through. The cabin she had rented was easy to find. It was the third one in the group of eight. The number read: *300*. The carport light burned as did a lamp in the front window. Once she drove into the carport she stopped, and for a long moment she laid her head on the steering wheel. *I don't know how an evening meeting with my new employer two days before Christmas became so crazy, but at least we made it here.. Thank you, God.*

Jenna blew out a big breath, and slid out of her car. Her legs and back were stiff from sitting so long, especially in a maximum state of stress. Stretching out, she pushed the key card into the kitchen door, and it opened easily. The next chore was carrying her in luggage, laptop, and the sacks of groceries she had purchased earlier in the afternoon. She glanced at the kitchen clock on the wall. Actually, it was yesterday, well past midnight.

CHAPTER THREE

"Excuse me. What?" He looked around "We've reached the cottage?" He stretched and winced at the stiffness, in his shoulder and arm. He felt the frigid air curling in from the raised back hatch. He carefully eased out of the car, and shuffled into what he decided, as he looked around, a *very* proper kitchen. To the left, he noticed an eating area tucked into a bay window. To the right was the food preparation oval, with all the modern appliances.

Through an archway he could see a living room, and on the wall straight ahead, a wood burning fireplace. It was set with wood, kindling, and paper, ready to be lighted. He stepped around a long sofa and checked the mantle and found fireplace matches. Bending over and with his right hand, he felt for the damper, opened it, and struck a flame. Even though he was very uncomfortable, he smiled as the fire caught, and flames danced up to the wood. He grinned in pleasure at seeing a real wood fire. Something that was rare in the British Isles.

He turned and watched Jenna wheel a suitcase into what likely was a bedroom. She returned to shut the kitchen door. "I'll find the thermostat and get some heat on. Great, you started the fire. I love a wood burning fireplace." She marched down the hall, probably to a bathroom.

Soon she returned. "The bathroom's down the hall. When you've freshened up, come into the kitchen, I want to take a look at your shoulder."

"Right on." He struggled up from the sofa and went down a short hall that was located behind the kitchen. When he returned, he noticed she had pulled a kitchen chair into the middle of the room, directly under the light fixture. She had removed her coat. Next, she slipped out of a gray wool jacket, and rolled up the sleeves of a red silk blouse.

She tapped the back of the chair with her hand. "Stand up please, but first we have to remove your jacket. I'm amazed you managed to get it back on."

The right sleeve came off easily, but blood from the wound had stuck his shirt to the jacket lining of the left sleeve. His shirt was stuck to the bandage the doctor had wrapped around his shoulder. She found a cloth and soaked it in warm water and wiped up inside of his sleeve as much as possible. "Keep standing." She gently rolled the jacket from his arm. "Now, your shirt." Again, she soaked the sleeve of his blue shirt until it came free of his arm.

There was some pain from the removal of his clothes. He bit his lip, and tried not to pull away from her ministrations. Strangely, an old memory of a childhood accident came to mind. He had been ice skating, fallen, and broken his leg. An above the boot top fracture, the doctors called it. Under his blue shirt he wore a sleeveless tee shirt. It was nearly free of blood stains.

She ran water in the sink, and came with a fresh bowl of water, and gently cleaned his arm. "The doctor thought your wound was a 'through and through?" She picked up his jacket and stuck her finger through the back of the left sleeve. "That would indicate the bullet went through you. I suppose a sling would be a good idea." She continued to pack the wound, and then taped it. She then went to a drawer in the kitchen area and found a large, white dish towel. She folded it into a sling, and wrapped it around his arm and shoulder.

"Among your other talents, are you also a nurse?" He asked.

She seemed to study him, and with large, cornflower blue eyes. She was amazing, and pretty too. He began to realize how fortunate he was that he had managed to jump into _her_ car.

"No, though I took a medical assistant's course in high school. I thought about medicine, but didn't have the math and science background to study it." She cleared her throat. "Now, I have some large sized ibuprofen. Do you have any problems with that drug? You will probably need a pain reliever when the shot wears off."

"No, not if it will keep the pain under control. No, I'm fine ingesting that drug."

"Good I'll make us some tea. You do drink tea, don't you?" She grinned down at him.

"That's next to 'mothers' milk to an Englishman." He felt his face actually crease into a smile.

She set the tea kettle on to boil, a blue kettle. He sat there hoping he could handle a cup of hot tea.

A few minutes later she set two cups of tea on the table and one large pill. It was only tea from a bag, but it tasted wonderful. He watched her soak and wash his blue shirt in the sink and then hang it to dry on a hook by the kitchen door.

"I don't know about you, but I'm bushed. It's been a rather eventful evening." She tilted her head and her mouth curved into tiny smile. "I made up your bed on the larger sofa. Let the fire die. It will be warm enough in here soon for sleeping. Do you need help getting out of your slacks?"

"If you unfasten my belt, I can do the rest." He felt his face warm as she efficiently did that chore, too. When she touched him, he reacted to her as he would any attractive woman. It was strange, even with a wounded shoulder that he now could think of her as sexually interesting.

He found she had taken time to open up the sofa bed. There were two pillows at the head and blankets spread across its surface. He eased down, but managed to stretch out and pull up a blanket.

*****

She snapped off the kitchen light, and he heard her walk behind the sofa, and a few seconds later the bedroom door close. He eased into his bed, and shifted the pillows to find some comfort for his shoulder. As he lay there and stared into the flames, he thought about this bazaar, actually insane evening. Why would some enemy want to kill him for the plans to a new type of *Battery?* It wasn't a blue print for a new missile trigger mechanism, or a trigger for a bomb. Just a large battery, extraordinary though it was. His eyes burned and he couldn't keep them open.

He wasn't sure if he heard her come and stand near his bed and look down on him. He heard the snap of the lamp in the corner of the living room, and the room became nearly dark.. Some moments later he again heard her close the bedroom door.

*****

It took Jenna a long time to fall asleep. What was she doing here, in her usually well-ordered life with this man? Now she had taken responsibility for a gunshot wounded, Brit? He seemed harmless enough, but was he? What was she going to with him, for him? He seemed to have found the sleep they both needed.

She did some breathing exercises that usually took away the day's tension, and worries. She found a comfortable position in the queen-sized bed. She'd be like Scarlett O'Hara, one of her favorite heroines, and worry about it tomorrow. Or at least when it was morning.

*****

Alistair awoke to the mouth-watering aroma of bacon frying and coffee brewing. Pushing up from the sofa bed took some serious maneuvering. His shoulder was stiff and radiated pain, and his whole body ached. However, he managed to grab his slacks and stumble into the bathroom. A few minutes later he emerged with face washed and hair combed.

He walked into the kitchen, and the sight of Jenna at the stove made his heart beat quicken. She was fresh and beautiful, with her blonde hair pulled into a pony tail. She wore a gray woolen sweater and heavy pants tucked into snow boots. Amazed, that he had stumbled across a girl so positive and special. It had been pure good fortune. Somehow, God in his Heaven, or a special Angel was looking out for him. He could almost feel Jenna's strength radiating to him, even in this unbelievable situation he found himself.

She turned and smiled. "Did you sleep well?" She went back to stirring the contents of the frying pan.

"Good morning. Surprisingly, yes, I did. I'm shocked how well. What are you preparing for breakfast?" At the word breakfast, his stomach growled. To him it sounded like thunder. And he slapped his good hand against his mid-section.

"Bacon, eggs, cinnamon rolls. Do you want coffee or tea?" She asked.

"Coffee. We Brits like our caffeine from that beverage in the morning, and I suppose tea the rest of the day. Although your soda drinks have made inroads into our habits." *Why are you prattling on like an idiot, Alistair?*

She set a mug of the brew on the table next to tableware and a napkin. "How do you like your eggs?"

"Oh, scrambled would be nice." He sat down and sipped the coffee. "This is a very nicely done kitchen. Clever, with a padded bench built into the bay window. I find the color scheme, attractive too. Dark red and navy blue, even mixed in with cream squares on the floor." He twisted to glance out the window. "The sun is up and shining!"

"Did you think the storm would last forever?" She turned to dish up a heaping plate of eggs, bacon, and a large, freshly iced cinnamon roll. She set it down in front of him. She also went to the refrigerator, grabbed a carton, poured two glasses of orange juice, and brought them to the table. "You must have your vitamin C." She grinned and set another plate of food and a mug of coffee across from him.

After taking a large mouthful of perfectly scrambled egg, he said. "You're wearing snow boots. Are you planning to go outside?"

"I've already been out there. It's beautiful and invigorating, but oh, so very cold. I love the winter. Where I grew up, it was an area of high desert. It did get cold, but not very often did we see any snow. I've been living in California for the past few years. No real winter there. That's one of the reasons why I took the position in this new company and moved to Utah."

"So, you enjoy this nearly arctic climate?" He shivered.

"You're feeling the cold, because you are sitting there in your underwear. Just a minute." She jumped up and ran to the hall. He heard her open a door. She returned quickly. "Here, stand up." She held out a heavy, plaid shirt. "Put your arm in the sleeve. Now drape it around your wounded arm. Good."

"That does warm me up a bit. Where did you find the shirt?"

"It was hanging in the hall closet. Someone must have left it. It doesn't quite fit you. You're taller and leaner than the individual who owned this shirt, but it will keep you comfortable for now." Quietly, efficiently, she finished eating, stood and began clearing the table. "Finish your breakfast. I need to finish my work. The light is better in here than at the little desk in the living room." She reached into her pocket and handed him another pill, a twin to the one she had given him the night before." Another pill for pain. Take it with you breakfast."

"What work must you do at this Holiday season?"

"I'll tell you what I'm going to be working on, but first you must tell me who and why people were chasing you and me last evening." She put her hands on her hips and arched an eyebrow.

"I can't tell you who or why, because I don't understand it myself. However, I'll get the disc that I think they wanted, and you may be able to draw some conclusions once you've seen it."

Chapter Four

"Okay, I'll go get my computer, and you go find, what a disc?"

She had set up her laptop, and sat with the light from the window behind her. He handed her the computer disc in a neat little box. "This is what those thugs wanted from you?" Her eyes widened and she shook her head. "Let's take a look." She slipped the disc into her computer. It read:

Presentation by Reacher and Jamison

The RLL-x78 Extended life Battery

Up came schematics for a long-life battery. First a type to be used in computers, and two others for television monitors.

"Someone, or some group wants to kill you for the plans for these batteries!? What will they do, detonate a nuclear bomb?" She asked, her eyes wide.

"My company sent me to this western state of Utah to watch a demonstration and pick up this disc. My company: *World Wide Electronics*, Limited, designs and makes products for televisions and computers. We are planning on encapsulating these batteries into our equipment. We sell to third world countries, where electricity is unreliable, or non-existent much of the time. Our products must run on batteries. These long use power sources would make our products in great demand. The televisions would run two hundred to three hundred hours, and computers, eighty to one hundred before battery replacement."

"So, these products were developed here in Utah?" She asked.

"Yes, two engineering, actually graduates from the university in Provo, Utah formed a company. They have applied for patents. The demonstration was above expectations. I must deliver this disc to my company near London."

"What's to stop these bad guys from staking out the Salt Lake Airport for your departure, or when you make another connection in some city like New York, waiting for you to board an airliner to what, Heathrow? They could grab you at any of these places."

"I've come to the same conclusion." He nodded, and spread his right hand on the table top.

"I'm not due back in Salt Lake until Monday evening. I believe we're safe here." She put a hand on his arm. "Meanwhile, you can rest and start to heal."

"I know. Tomorrow is Christmas. I was hoping to, as ET would say, to 'phone home'." He tilted his head and tried for a smile.

"I know you'd like to do that, but using your cell phone would be dangerous. By the way, did you ever _find_ your cell phone? My phone does not have overseas capabilities. At any rate, it depends on how sophisticated your pursuers are. We're stuck here for a couple of days. We have plenty of firewood, and food."

"My cellular phone, no. By the way, this cottage has central heat, does it not?" He lifted an eyebrow.

"Yes, all the modern conveniences." She flashed a beautiful smile. "I was teasing. But you have to admit, a wood burning fire is festive." She slid out of the padded seat and brought over the carafe. "More coffee?"

"Yes, thank you. You wouldn't mind if I retired to sofa?"

"No, I'll make it up so you can sit up, and watch a movie on the TV. Right now, the satellite is out, but there is quite a selection of videos to choose from. They're on the book shelf, left of the fireplace." She turned to him. "Were you planning on celebrating Christmas with your wife, family, and friends?"

"No wife. With my Mum and Dad, and my sister, her husband and the two kids." They will be at the parents' house in York. I usually try to join them, at least on Christmas Day. But now I'm- - - - "

"You're here with me stuck in Utah. I _am_ sorry. Sorry you've been shot, and are being chased by an unknown enemy." She picked up his coffee. "Let's get you settled, and you can watch something cheerful." She walked into the living room and in a few minutes had the sofa bed folded back into a normal couch. She returned to the kitchen and helped him up,

He sat down, but took her hand. "I'm grateful to you for still being alive, and here, and full of a delicious breakfast." His green-brown eyes met her blue ones. "Pick something humorous. I need a lift."

She perused the group of DVD's. "How about _The Christmas Story_. It's an American classic. Or if you prefer, there is a version of Dickens's _Christmas Story_

"The American one." He reached with his right hand and snagged the mug of coffee.

She set up the disc, and handed him the remote. "Enjoy, I've many hours of work to do." She walked back into the kitchen.

He called out to her. "What are you working on?"

"A power point presentation of a new account. I'll let you see it, and you can critique it for me, later. I must have this ready by Tuesday, December twenty-seventh. Whoops, I almost forgot." She walked back into the living area and handed him several pills. "Another pill for pain, a muscle relaxant, and a vitamin C. Take the pain pill when you feel you need it again. Talk to you later."

Alistair arranged the pillows to ease the pain, and most comfort for his shoulder, clicked on the remote, and began to watch the video. Soon, though he grew sleepy, closed his eyes, and fell asleep.

*****

Less than an hour later, Jenna came into the living room to check on her house guest, and found him snoring softly. She eased off his shoes, covered him with a throw blanket, and clicked off the TV. There must be something more she could do to help him. She'd think on that later. Right now, she was moving along with her work, and did not want to lose focus on the presentation. She went back to kitchen and made another pot of coffee.

Hours later, she scooted out of the bench seat, stood up and stretched. She began to think how she could help Alistair? *It's better for both of us to turn him over to the authorities or- - --?* The thought bouncing around in her head was far out, but the idea nagged at her. She went to the bedroom for her cell phone, and dialed an old familiar number.

The voice on the other end answered. "Southern Dixie Animal Clinic, how may I help you?"

Jenna breathed a sigh of relief. "Is this Claire?"

"Yes, to whom am I speaking?" Jenna could hear the question and the professionalism in the woman's voice.

"It's Jenna, Jenna Barlow. I heard you were now running the animal clinic, and recently got married."

"Jenna, how and where are you? My goodness, how long has it been? You must have talked to Suzanne."

"I did. The reason why I called is that I have a rather unusual problem, and I thought you and your FBI husband could help me, us."

"You want to hire us? We charge, because we are now licensed investigators. And it's Christmas Eve. Does this mean you're in a serious jam?"

"I am well aware its Christmas Eve, but I got involved and rescued a guy. Much the same way I heard you and Suzy rescued Mac." She took a deep breath. "Let me start at the beginning." She went on to relate the events of the evening before and now where Alistair and she were.

"Wow Jenna, you don't do things half way, do you?" Claire was silent for a beat. "We're having a little Christmas party, here at the clinic in a few minutes. But I will call Mac, and run your story by him. I'll call you back later this evening."

"Thanks Claire. I do hate to bother you on Christmas, but I'm desperate."

"I promise I'll return your call. Meanwhile, Merry Christmas."

Jenna closed her phone and turned to stare out the kitchen window. The sun made the mounds of snow sparkle like tiny gems. She was suddenly grateful to be here, warm, *free* and now for Alistair's company on this Christmas Eve. She had planned to be alone this Holiday, yet she had purchased enough food for two? Why was that? She stepped outside and felt the deep winter cold, and the weak winter sun on her arms. She yawned and stepped back into the cottage. She glanced at her watch. It was nearly two P.M. After the events of last night, she could use a nap. She scooped up her cell phone and tip toed into the bedroom.

*****

Alistair woke with a start, cold and stiff and disoriented. He found he was on a sofa, in a dim room, a blank TV to the right, and a fireplace directly in his line of sight. He closed his eyes, and slowly the events of the past 24 hours came into focus. *Get up man, move, your blood is running cold and sluggish in your veins.* He stretched and pushed up with his right arm. His injured left shoulder felt numb rather than as painful as it had been before.

With slow awkward movements he began to build a fire, lighted it, and sat back to watch it flame. Tea, that's what he wanted. Once in the kitchen, he put on the kettle, and began the search for teabags.

Pulling himself up from the padded bench, he turned off the stove and poured steaming water into a mug, and carried it back to the table. He heard the jangle of a phone playing a Christmas tune. It must be Jenna's. Perhaps she would like a cup of tea, too.

She must in the bedroom. He knocked on the half open door, and found her sitting in the middle of a queen-sized bed, the phone to her ear. "Would you like some tea?" He spoke in a soft voice.

She nodded, and went on talking. A few minutes later she came into the kitchen. She took a sip of her tea, looked up at him and grinned. "We're going to have houseguests."

He frowned. "Where are they going to sleep?"

"In the loft. I'll need to check on the accommodations up there in a few minutes" She sipped her tea and grinned.

The stairway to the loft was tucked next to the wall outside of the Jenna's bedroom. "I must have a look." He walked into the living room, and stared at the narrow stairway leading up to an open loft area. Now he studied it, whereas before he had just glanced at it, not paying much attention. It seemed to be above the bedroom and the bathroom. When he felt a little stronger, he would have to go up for a look. For now, he went back to his tea.

CHAPTER FIVE

Alistair slid into his chair. "From what area of the state, are these houseguests coming?" He took a large swallow of tea. "And who are they?"

"I have a friend married to an FBI agent. They're coming tomorrow. I think they can help you, me, actually both of us. The best thing is to get you out of Utah and back to your homeland. They're driving up from a town close to St. George, Utah."

"They're traveling on Christmas Day? How far away is St. George? Isn't that unusual for even a good friend to travel such a distance on a Holiday such as Christmas?"

"From here, at Cole Cliffs Resort, possibly three hundred seventy or eighty miles. It depends on the route they decide to take." She shrugged. "I suppose it's unusual, but Mac is intrigued with your situation." She laughed. "My friend is Claire and he's Mac. MacCandlass is the last name."

His stomach growled loudly, and he put his hand over his stomach. "So sorry."

She tilted her head to look at the clock. "No wonder your stomach is protesting. It's after four P.M. Time to start dinner." She jumped up and opened the refrigerator, and began taking bags of food from it.

He watched her rinse a whole chicken, and prepare it for roasting. Next, she worked on a gelatin fruit salad, and after that, began to fix a box of stuffing.

"You planned to fix all this food for you to eat alone?" His eyes widened as he watched her.

She turned to him, her face rosy, from her food preparation. So alive, and so beautiful. "I still can't say why I bought so much food, but alone or not, I wanted a Christmas dinner. Now I have you as a guest to help me enjoy our Christmas bounty. Already my Holiday is better than I had planned." Her smile was sincere, and disarming, and she was so pretty. He felt a strong attraction to her, and his heart did a little flip.

"May I ask why you chose to be here, in this remote place. You planned to be alone at this special time of the year? Away from your family, and friends. Surely, there was someone with whom you would want to spend the time. People you'd like to be with, at Christmas?"

"My family, what's left of it, live further away than St. George. *and* I cannot return to my town.." She turned away and worked on the preparation of their dinner.

"What do you mean, you can't go back? Are they somewhere too far away?" He asked.

"They won't even let me in the town, much less to my family home." The expression on her face was so sad; it made Alistair's heart ache for her.

"What strange place would this be?" He frowned.

"It's on the Utah-Arizona border. The town is called River Mesa. The whole community is closed to anyone not living the 'principle'."

"The principle?" *What strange town would this be?*

"Polygamy. One man many wives. Another name for the group is the FLDS."

"You were in a polygamist relationship?" He couldn't believe what he was hearing.

"No, I was born to the fifth wife of a man who actually had six wives, and some twenty odd children, at last count anyway."

"I remember seeing expose/ programs on the television about polygamists, but I assumed the shows were a wildly exaggerated."

"That could be, but believe me it's a bizarre lifestyle." She turned back to the construction of her dressing and placed it into a baking pan.

"So, what were the circumstances of your leaving the town, may I ask?'

She stood facing the kitchen counter for a long moment, and as she turned, her eyes were filled with tears. *I suppose I can share my strange family, upbringing with him. In a few days, I'll never see him again..* "My mother gave birth to me when she was 39 years old. I was her sixth child. Two-and a half years later she had another girl named Jasmine. When I turned fourteen, I was betrothed to a man who was 49 years old, and already had 4 wives. My mother became ill so the wedding was postponed. The elders did allow my mom to see a doctor. The diagnosis was breast cancer. They did the surgery, but her husband would not allow chemo or radiation."

"Why did they not allow the complete treatment?' Alistair asked.

"The first and most compelling reason is that she would lose her hair. In the FLDS religion, a woman never cuts her hair. It's because she must have hair long enough to wash her husband's feet with it. When they all die and reach Heaven, especially." She rolled her eyes. "The second reason was money and the chemo treatments would take her away from the town. And into the apostate, evil world."

"How strange." He shook his head. "The leaders of your town believed that the rest of the world was evil?"

Jenna nodded, and glanced down at the floor. "She died six months after the surgery. She suffered so much." Tears tracked down her cheeks; "Even though I tried my best to take care of her."

He stood up from his chair and moved to her, but she whirled around away from him. "I must check the chicken." She checked the dressing pan in the oven. She stared at the stove for a long moment, but as she turned, he embraced her.

"I'm so sorry." He whispered into her hair. They stood for a several seconds, as he held her awkwardly. Slowly she pushed away, and slid into a chair near the table. "So how did you escape?" He asked.

"After my mother's funeral, my wedding was again scheduled for a Saturday three weeks later. My wedding day came, and I was spiritually married to this older man. All I could think of was that

I didn't want to marry him or anyone else. I didn't want to live that life, to be married to man who I couldn't stand to even be near.

Through happenstance, I had the marvelous opportunity to leave the wedding and run back to my room. I gathered up some things and went out to the highway and began to walk to St. George.

I've always thought that if I married, I would get breast cancer, or some other disease that comes from having children. I worried about my little sister, but she was only twelve, and had a few more years before she would be forced to marry some older man.

There are still women in St. George that will take in a runaway girl from River Mesa. They make up flyers and drop them, scattering the papers on the road. Sometimes we would see them tacked to power poles. Some of the girls would gather them up and we'd pass them around. On the papers were phone numbers.

As I mentioned, my wedding happened. It went on as planned. The sister wives of my family fixed a dress for me and a veil. I was 'spiritually' married to the man who had chosen me. There was a celebration with dinner and dancing. My new husband was called away for a while, and I took advantage of his absence to run away.

The woman who put out the flyers just happened to be driving on the highway that evening. Somehow that night she came by, and offered me a ride, and I hopped into her car. When we reached her house, there were two other girls living there with her. They also had run away."

"She took you back to St George?" He asked.

"Yes, she took me in, enrolled me in the local high school. The next morning, she fixed a good breakfast. In her basement were stacks of clothes, normal clothes, like jeans and tee shirts, sneakers and jackets. Legally, it was easy for her to become my foster mother, because I had no legal relative to claim me.

The state of Utah would have loved to storm the Polygamous town, and take all the children into foster care, but Arizona would have to be involved in the raid, too. The costs to both states would have been millions in housing and court costs. At least this way the law was on our side. It was legal for any girl or boy for that matter, to escape. Anyone who wanted out of the life style." She explained.

"What about the teenage boys? Could they leave as easily?"

"They came to have the name 'Lost Boys' because they are kicked out. They were too much competition to the older men for a young girl's affection, but not all of them. If a boy has a father that needs him to work at some business, or shows talent in construction, or auto repair and would follow in their father's beliefs, they were allowed to stay."

"What happens to the boys that are kicked out?" Alistair stared at her and his mind still whirled. He felt as if he were in mild shock. *This is a terrible story and worse place where these children must live.*

"There are some group homes for them, too. But they run into trouble. They are shunned in high school, mainly because they haven't been able to develop an athletic skill. In most high schools in the U.S. an athletic skill gives a boy status. So lost boys take to drinking and drugs, which are plentiful in a border town like St. George. I've heard of a few success stories, but not many."

"Why don't more of the girls run away? Sorry, but I am curious about this strange lifestyle."

"They brainwash you. You're told that if you run away, you'll end up in a brothel in Las Vegas, or at the very least you'll be cleaning hotel rooms for the rest of your life. When you die, you'll automatically go to Hell."

"I'm curious. What type of clothes did you wear in the town where you lived? You spoke of normal teenage clothing being different." He tilted his head and frowned.

"Nineteenth Century dresses. Oprah named them Prairie Dresses. Long sleeved, to the ankle, homemade underwear. And of course your hair in a long braid, because you were never allowed to cut it."

"Why were you forced to wear long underwear?" He wished he had a way to take notes, this story was so weird.

"It is supposedly sacred underwear. Main stream Mormons, if they have visited a Temple wear them, but they are skimpy, compared to what we were forced to wear."

"Did you go to school in St. George?"

"Yes, we were enrolled immediately. I went into the ninth grade and Fern was in the tenth. Regular school was a big surprise. We soon found out the FLDS curriculum we had been taught, was a pack of lies, or full of distortions."

"We were told that if we did runaway, and went to regular high school, we would be grabbed and mauled by the boys there. But we soon found out that most of them thought we were too strange to even come near. Suzanne and Claire were popular and a grade ahead of Fern. They decided to befriend us. They helped us to study, to learn to use the computer, and became our campus guardians."

Chapter Six

"Did your father try to come after you?" Alistair wanted to know more, how this lovely girl escaped such a strange and possibly damaging childhood.

"No, sometimes I wonder if they don't believe their own lies. He probably decided that I had ended up a hooker in Las Vegas or a cocktail waitress."

"How close is Las Vegas?" He asked.

"Two hours from St. George."

The oven timer began to beep. "I'll check on our dinner." Yes, now it's time for the rolls to go into the oven."

*****

The time for intimate conversation had vanished, and Jenna returned to preparing their Christmas Dinner. She set the table, and took a bottle of wine from the refrigerator. "Do you want to start with tea, or wine?" She smiled, straightened her sweater, and carried a platter of chicken and dressing to the table. She brought out the rest of their feast, To Alistair it was as festive as if there were to be many guests invited instead of just the two of them. In this Holiday atmosphere they began their Christmas feast.

After eating more than he should have, Alistair pushed his chair back from the table. "That was a wonderful Christmas Eve dinner, thank you for preparing it."

"You go into the living area, while I clean up. Just relax." Jenna smiled and began clearing the table.

He walked in and stirred the fire. What caught his eye was the small round table by the front bay window. On it was a tree, possibly three feet in height. Though it was artificial, it was a perfectly shaped evergreen. It stood on a red Christmas patterned, circular cloth that draped to the floor. His attention now drifted to a book shelf. He noticed a cupboard on the left side, below the shelf of books. He opened it to see what was inside, and found Christmas lights, and other tree decorations. He emptied the shelf and set the boxes on the sofa, he couldn't stop a smile.

"Jenna, come see what I found. I finally noticed this little tree. Because of its shape: It's an evergreen. It could be a Christmas tree, and here are the trimmings." He picked up a box of lights and held them up.

She came in wiping her hands on a towel. "Well, isn't that interesting. I noticed the tree on the table, but never really studied it." She took the package of tiny colored lights. A smile brightened her face. "I think we should decorate it, don't you?'

Soon, she had the strand of lights artfully placed on the tree. Alistair sat on the sofa, and handed her the colored glass balls one at the time. First, she put on ornaments of red, and then he handed her the contents of another box. In this box were green Christmas ornaments. Inside the cupboard he noticed another small box.

"Grab the small box." Jenna said. In it was a beautiful multicolored, glass bird, with a clip under his body. "He belongs on the top." Jenna clipped the ornament on the top of the tree. Alistair pulled out a roll of ribbon from between the cushions. "Here is some ribbon."

She draped the ribbon on the little tree and stood back. "Well, that didn't take very long, and I love a Christmas Tree, any size." She leaned over and kissed Alistair on his cheek. "Thank you for finding the decorations. I'll be back in a moment." She returned carrying two wine glasses, and the bottle of chardonnay. She poured some wine in each of the glasses and sat down next to Alistair. With his right hand he reached over and picked up her left hand. "My, such a small appendage for all the work it does."

"Appendage?" She sat up and stared at him. "Where did that word come from?'"

"My days in physiology courses. I thought of becoming an exercise physiologist, but computer technology lured me away. That and computer technology pays more pounds per week in salary."

"Did you major in computers in college?" She asked.

"Not entirely, I took courses in this and that, some in engineering. When I took the position with *World Wide Electronics,* I'd had a number of employment experiences. I went to work for WWE, Limited, about five years ago." He said.

"Now would you share with me how you managed move from the group home in St. George, to being employed in an advertising agency? Oh, also. How did your community get that name?" He continued.

"You mean St. George? It's named after George Washington, our first president, I believe. And because the town is in Washington County. Rather obvious." She laughed.

"I went to high school there, and junior college. Next I found a job in a coffee shop to earn money and applied for a scholarship at Southern Utah University."

"Any romantic liaisons during your college years?" He glanced at her and took a sip of his wine.

"I vowed to stay away from men for a time. When I lived in River Mesa, men seemed to be the root of all my problems. Besides, I had to keep up my grades to maintain my scholarship. I never had enough money for party dresses, or even good clothes to wear to church, so I avoided both men and religion. However, I did start out to be in a medical field, but I took a course called <u>The Influence of Advertising,</u> which I found fascinating. So, I began filling out the basic course requirements and applied for a Pell Grant, and got it."

"What is a Pell Grant? Some kind of financial help with tuition?"

"Yes, I received full tuition and books, as well as a break on a dorm room costs. It saved me a lot of money." She turned, and picked up her wine and studied him for a beat. "What about you? You're in your 30's, right? What about romantic entanglements in your life?"

"I lived with a girl for a time, and thought about marriage. She had other plans for her life. She wanted to travel, and applied for a teaching position in the Czech Republic. That was one of the reasons I went to London, and found the position I have now. York is a large city, but not like London. Did you find conditions living in Los Angeles, California, in that large city, to your liking?" He turned the conversation back to Jenna.

"I didn't live in Los Angeles. I always wanted to live near the beach. I lucked out, because one of the secretaries where I worked had an apartment near the beach. It was located about two blocks from the ocean in Venice Beach. I sublet it from her, totally furnished.

Parking however, is a major problem in a beach city, but I finally found a spot I could rent about a half a block from where I lived. From time to time the secretary would come and collect some of her furnishings, which gave me a chance to replace them with things that were more to my taste. Living in Los Angeles County, traffic is the big problem, but you adjust. Some mornings I could get into work in 20 minutes. Other days it took twice that long. How did you manage in London?"

"I took the 'tube'. It took half an hour at least, in transport." Is there a subway in Los Angeles?"

"No, just freeways and endless traffic. Do you know that there is a vehicle registered in Los Angeles County for every one point four people living there? After I worked at my first job for about four years, I jumped companies to Alta- Angeles. It was closer to my apartment, too."

"You Americans have an interesting way to communicate. 'Jump companies'? I do believe I understand what you said, in the context of the sentence." He followed his comment with a smile.

"If you're going be dealing with us 'backwoods' Westerners, you'd better get used to our idioms." She laughed, and moved over to the end of the sofa, so she could look at his face, or at least that was what he told himself.

Then she asked. "Why in the world is a great looking guy like you not married?"

"The fact that you consider me 'great looking' pleases me." He thought for a moment, and cleared his throat. "I was married until about four years ago. First, we separated, Belinda and me. With this new job, I worked long hours. I would come home and find her gone. I would need to search for her in the local pubs, and find her downing pints and singing. I'd not been brought up to enjoy that type of entertainment." He scowled at the floor.

"I'm sorry. Were you and Belinda married long?" She gave him an understanding nod.

"About two-and-a-half years. She worked in the cosmetic industry. She was talented at what she did, and found a job closer to London. I was hoping she'd want children, but many English women don't seem interested in motherhood anymore."

"What about you. Aren't you close to thirty years of age?" No serious romances?" He asked.

"Yes, well- - - - - - - -," She played with a lock of her hair and studied her lap, but then glanced at the TV. "Do you mind if we check to see if we can pick up the ten o'clock news."

He shook his head and smiled. *Interesting way to evade the question.* "No, go ahead."

✳✳✳✳✳

She grabbed up the remote and flipped through some channels until she came to the NBC affiliate. The first story had to do with a house fire. But the second story caught her attention.

The Anchor man said: *Earlier today, it was reported that shots were fired last evening in Cottonwood Heights, and led to an arrest of two foreign nationals. Police are still searching for the car they fired on. The men were detained and their car searched. Two semi-automatic weapons were confiscated. They refused to say why they fired the weapons, or at who. One of the men, a North Korean National has diplomatic immunity.*

The second is here on a student visa at Brigham Young University, but both remain in jail until their court hearing on Monday morning. After paying a fine, both of them could be deported. If anyone knows anything about this incident, please call the Holiday-Cottonwood Police at this number. The car fired upon was a white or silver colored, late model Lexus. No information on its owner.

"Oh my gosh, those thugs are North Koreans? Wow, this is turning into an international incident." Her eyes widened as she stared at him.

"Hmmm, at least we won't don't need to worry about those two. We know where they are. North Koreans, I'm now beginning to understand as to why they would want the disc. But why steal it from me? They could have purchased it from the inventors."

"Maybe they didn't want to *pay_*for it, because of the patent rights. They didn't want the guys in Provo, and your company in London to know they had the schematics. That country causes so much chaos. I don't know if we, as a nation, are allowed to legally even do business with them." Jenna said.

He stood, winced, and cradled his left arm against his chest. "I'm making tea. Do you want some?"

She nodded, but turned her attention back to the news program. When he returned with the tea, she was making up his sofa bed. "Here's another pill." She handed it to him. "I can see your arm is causing you pain. Rest is important for the healing process."

He sat in one of two wing chairs by the table holding the Christmas tree. "I hope I can sleep."

"You need to have another glass of wine. That will relax you. Hang on, I have dessert." She went back into the kitchen, and soon returned, and set a plate with a slice of ice cream roll on the small table next to him.

"Where did this come from?" He forked up a bite

"I found it in the freezer. The owner of these cottages left it as a Christmas treat for us." She sat down, sipped her tea and tried a bite of the cake.

"This is delicious. I love dessert, especially ice cream." He took another large forkful.

"I should finish up the dishes." She picked up the plates and wine glasses, finishing off the little bit left it hers. She heard the television program change to one of a choir singing, classical Christmas music.

CHAPTER SEVEN

"This is a proper program to view on Christmas Eve." He said.

"Yes, it is." She stood for moment leaning against the back of the sofa bed. She walked into her bedroom, but a few minutes later she came out wearing a gray robe and, fuzzy pink slippers. She sat on the love seat and seemed to be listening to the music.

He thought about Christmas Eve at his parents' house with his sister, her husband and the two little ones. He also thought about calling his superior, Winn Carruthers, and informing him of his plight. Yet, he understood how easily the signal from a cell phone could be tracked, and he definitely did not want any harm to come to Jenna. He would be forced to wait.

Where was his cellular phone anyway? He had forgotten about it until now. He's look through his briefcase for it later. Perhaps this Mac, fellow could help him to safely return to London along with the disc.

She stood, and walked around to him. "It's after eleven, and tomorrow comes along early. Try to sleep. When Claire and Mac arrive, the four of us, may be able to solve this dilemma of yours quickly and simply."

She was so attractive, appealing, and he found he wanted to be close to her. He stood and slid his good arm around her and drew her in for a kiss. His motive was to keep it sweet and gentle, but she sighed into his mouth, and he deepened the kiss. Her scent was of spicy cologne, mixed with the aroma of the food she had cooked. He became aroused and wanted her. But in reality, with his painful, wounded arm he would be, at that moment in time, quite a poor lover.

She gently backed away from him but he caught her hand. "I want to thank you for saving me, for sheltering and fixing delicious food for me. A Christmas dinner I'm not likely to forget," he said.

Her eyes held his. "I couldn't do anything else." She hugged him for a long moment, and rested her chin on his shoulder. Then she brushed her hand across his back and moved away.

He closed his eyes, and when he opened them, she was gone. He sat back down in the blue wing chair and stared out the window at the mounds of snow across from the cottage. Then he stood close to the window, staring, but not out and thought about that first Christmas Eve in Bethlehem, so long ago. Even then the world was dominated by the warriors, thieves, and self-righteous men who wouldn't recognize that a special man among them had been sent from God, they had their own selfish goals. Not much had changed in over 2000 years.

Alistair slept later than the morning before. Once he stood up, it took a long moment to shake his strange dream. He dreamed that the Baby Jesus had been born in the snow, and it was up to Alistair to rescue him, along with the infant's mother and father. Finally, he brought them into the cottage and moved them near the fire.

While washing up in the bathroom, he shook his head, as he thought of the possible origin of the dream. It was Christmas morning after all, and he could relate to the little family far away from their home town, and could only find a stable for shelter. Now over 2000 years later, a man could rejoice because of that humble birth. He wasn't a religious man, yet the fact of Christ's divinity comforted him.

He went into the kitchen and found breakfast, but no Jenna. Perhaps she had gone for a walk. He stepped out into the carport and found her standing quietly on that cold, bright morning. "Good morning." She turned, and surprise flickered across her lovely face. "Alistair, it's too cold for you to be out here."

"And not too chilly for you?" He walked to her and wrapped his good arm around her back, and crossed it around her waist. "Now we'll have the body heat of two." He chuckled close to her ear.

She turned in his arms, kissed him on the cheek, then took his hand, and pulled him back to the warmth of the kitchen. "I came out here to study the bullet hole damage to my car." She tilted her head and frowned. 'Come, let's go in and eat breakfast." The mouthwatering aroma of cinnamon, and the ding of the stove timer, brought him to the range. "Move, let me get out the apple-cinnamon bread. Sit down." She poured a mug of coffee and handed it to him.

"You're a wonderful cook. Do you prepare food like this a regular basis?'

"No, I suppose it's because I bought all the food, and now you're here for me to feed. I'm enjoying myself." She grinned, and set a small plate on the table, with half a pink grapefruit on it.

"Ah, more vitamin C." He spooned up a section. "What are your plans for this morning?"

"I still have some work to do for my presentation. So I'd better finish it now. Once Claire and Mac arrive, we'll be involved with what they can do to help you."

"I'd like to take a walk. I'm used to walking several blocks each day. I suppose I'm restless." He took a bite of the warm bread.

"Mr. Crawford came over and plowed a path. I'm not sure about your shoes. You may slip and slide in those things." She frowned, and glanced down at his loafers.

"I'll take my chances. I will need for you to help me into my jacket." He hoped she would go with him.

"Okay, let's clean up breakfast. I'll work a few hours, and then we'll try a walk. It may be a little warmer outside later." She put her hand on his arm.

While Jenna worked, he found a novel by Vince Flynn. An American writer he had no experience reading before. It turned out to be an international thriller. But sometime later, he became sleepy, and abandoned the book for a nap.

Jenna finally finished her presentation about mid afternoon, and was happy to turn off her computer. She hoped Mac would be able to help Alistair, and arrange for him to return to London, safely. She hoped Claire would have some meds to heal her house guest's shoulder.

Jenna went outside, and even with her heavy coat, she felt the winter chill. The sun was dropping low in the western sky, and with it down went the temperature. She turned around and started back to the cottage when she saw Alistair walking toward her. "Are you warm enough to be outside?" His cheeks were red, and his nose looked like it was running.

"I managed to put my jacket over this heavy shirt, but I would have liked to have some gloves." He shivered, but tried for a smile. "I have a warm coat, gloves and a cap in my hotel room."

"Let's go back. You need move than gloves to be out here." She took his arm. "Are you hungry?"

"I'm always hungry." He laughed, but then shivered again.

"Come on." She opened the kitchen door. "I'll make you some cheese toast. Let me help you get out of that jacket." She tugged at the dark brown sleeve.

"I came out to tell you that you had a phone call. It was from Claire. She said to tell you she's bringing supper."

He sat down at the table and watched her make the cheese toast, and put the kettle on for tea. The cheese toast was tasty, and easily done in the microwave He would try and remember how to do that snack when he reached his flat in London.

"They probably won't arrive here for another hour or two. Meanwhile, I'm taking a nap, because Claire and I may be up for hours gossiping about our old friends in St. George." She stood, wiped off the kitchen counter, and walked into the bedroom.

The December dark had fallen when an older Subaru station wagon pulled into the carport behind Jenna's car. A few moments later the front door bell jangled, and Jenna ran to the door and threw it open. "Claire!" Jenna pulled her friend into the living area, and gave her a big hug.

Behind her stood a red-haired man, about the same height as Alistair. "You must be Mac." She stood back allowing him to enter. Walking into the kitchen she said. "Mac, Claire, this is Alistair." He stood awkwardly, and pushed out of the chair where he had been sitting. He stuck out his right hand and Mac shook it.

"Come, bring in your things." Jenna motioned to the kitchen door. She watched as they both stomped back out to the Subaru, and began taking bags and small suitcases from it, along with a extra large pizza.

"Set the oven temp to 400 F. Jenna we need to bake this." Claire slipped the large pie from its box and set it into the oven.

After they had all eaten their fill, Mac sat back on his chair and sipped his ice tea. "May I see the disc that the North Koreans wanted enough to kill you to get it?" He glanced at Alistair, tilted his head, and his mouth twitched.

Jenna carried in her laptop, and brought Alistair's briefcase to him. He fished out the disc and handed it to Mac. He booted up the computer and studied the disc for several minutes. The other three sat in silence.

Finally, Claire stood, and took a chair out into the middle of the kitchen. "Alistair, let me take a look at your shoulder." Jenna helped him take off the sling and his blue shirt. Claire turned to Jenna, "Yep, as you predicted there is some infection, but all in all Jenna you did a good job. I'll bet it hurts like hell."

"Oh Al, you should have said something." Jenna had a stricken look on her face.

"What could I say?" You gave me pain pills, and did the best you could under the circumstances." Alistair said.

"We'll fix you up." Claire went for a medical bag and took out a spray bottle. "This is going to be cold, but your shoulder will be numb in 30 seconds."

He winced when the frigid spray hit his hot, swollen skin, but as she predicted the area went numb quickly. She worked cleaning the wound, and soon had new bandages on it. Jenna helped him back into his shirt and sling, but left it open. Claire handed him his iced tea and two pills.

"Take these now, but as a precaution, I am giving you a penicillin shot to jump start the medication in your blood stream. You aren't allergic to penicillin, are you?"

Alistair shook his head. "No, not that I'm aware."

Jenna slid his shirt down on his right arm.

"I'm putting the injection in your right shoulder." Claire prepared the injection site and did as she had promised. It stung only for a moment.

Alistair went back to the table and sat down slowly. Perhaps if he sat quietly, and breathed slowly, he could ease the pain in both of his shoulders. For a long moment he studied Claire. She was taller than Jenna by three or four inches. She seemed strong and muscular, but also slim. Yet in her own way she was very attractive, with short brown hair and light brown eyes.

*****

Mac glanced up. "These are amazing batteries. Are they really as good as the information on the disc describes? I can see why the North Koreans or any other hostile nation would like to get their hands on this disc. Already I can see these batteries could be used in beneficial and definitely hostile ways."

Chapter Eight.

"The two-day demonstration I witnessed seemed to support their long life and reliability. When I called the factory in London, our operations man was excited to try and for me to purchase some of the batteries and install, them into our products." Alistair said.

"Two questions. First, who would you think may be the traitor to or in your company? I believe there are millions of dollars, and or pounds, etc. to be made here. Two, where is your hotel room, and what did you leave in it?" Mac studied Alistair with penetrating green eyes.

"A mole in the company? I have thought and thought as to who would benefit from illegal activities. Those with the most to gain would be Carruthers in operations, or the CEO, Rutledge." Al sat back and took a deep breath. "My hotel room is number 325 at the Sheraton, and the key is in my jacket pocket. My passport is in the safe. I'll write down the combination."

"Okay, I'll go with the supposition that it could be one of those two guys you mentioned." He turned to Jenna. "Are you familiar with that hotel?"

"Yes, I'm supposed to check in there tomorrow evening. Why?"

"Because, you and I are going down there right now and clean out Alistair's room. So, get your coat and the key." Mac said. "Oh, and wear something that looks like Christmas."

"Okay." She nodded. "Good thinking, Mac. Obviously, Alistair can't go anywhere without his passport and belongings."

Before they left, Mac and Jenna went out to check the bullet damage to her car. "You two were so lucky, that all you have is a shattered mirror and a bullet hole in your back hatch. They could have taken you 'out'. You or Al or both of you." Mac shook his head.

"I'm going to let you drive, Jenna. I have a headache, and it won't go away until I get some sleep." They got into the car, and Jenna drove down the long lane and picked up the freeway heading west. "I can see how you dodged those bad guys. You are quite the skilled driver." Mac said.

Once they reached the freeway, the roads had been cleared, and they could drive at freeway speeds. They made good time, and when they reached the hotel, Jenna backed the car into a spot. She chose the west side of the hotel, with the car facing a west entrance. Mac could see a doorway into a hall across the parking lot.

"Okay, I'm going into the front door and walk through the lobby. There may be a Christmas party going on, so I'll ease through it, and come to that door and let you in. It may take me a few minutes." Jenna said.

Jenna strolled into the hotel lobby toward the 20-foot Christmas tree standing against the tall windows facing north. One of the secretaries from Alta-Angeles called to her. "Hey Jenna, Merry Christmas. I thought you wouldn't be back in town until Tuesday."

"You're right. I'll be back here tomorrow. I left a couple of things in the hotel safe. They're little gifts for some friends." She lied. She walked over to the desk and then around it. She took a deep breath and eased over to an employee behind the desk. His employee badge read: Rick.

"May I help you?" He asked.

'Yes, I have a reservation for tomorrow afternoon. Would you happen to know which room I'll be in?" He went to the computer.

"No, but you'll be on the fourth floor as you requested." He smiled at her.

"Thanks, I'll go check it out. She went down the hall and checked to make sure no one was in the corridor. Quickly she opened the heavy glass door to the outside. A few seconds later, Mac walked from the car and into the hallway. The elevator is this way." She took his arm.

As they stepped out on level three, they were forced to walk by a group of people standing in an open room doorway, some with drinks in their hands. "Great, a party." Mac grumbled.

"Hi Jenna, come join us." A guy staggered into the hallway waving a glass. "Bring your friend along, too."

"Maybe a little later." She took Mac's arm and hugged him tight against her. "You got the key, lover?" She looked up into Mac's eyes.

Mac took Alistair's key from his coat pocket, and pushed it into the lock. "Later guys, much later." He flashed a lascivious grin in the direction of the group, opened the hotel room, and shoved Jenna into the darkened room, slamming the door.

The only light in the room came from the window and the street light below. Jenna snapped on the bathroom light, while Mac closed the drapes. He went to the desk and turned on the lamp. "Here's Alistair's laptop." You get his clothes and I'll search the room."

Jenna located Alistair's brown suitcase and began filling it with clothes and toiletries. Within ten minutes they had finished a thorough search, and packed up everything that could belong to Alistair Powell. "Ready to leave?"

"Yes, but first, check the hall." Mac ordered.

Jenna cracked the door open and couldn't see anyone standing outside the door, but the opposite door was open with music, voices, and raucous laughter coming from the room. "Clear." She said.

Mac picked up the valise, while Jenna took the laptop and a heavy coat. They exited quickly, and closed the door as quietly as possible. Once they were in the elevator, Mac turned to Jenna. "You'd make a good operative. You think and act fast on your feet."

"I suppose I can give a few spy novels and TV some credit." She laughed.

As the elevator opened and they stepped out, a tall dark, haired man came down the hall. "Jenna?" he said.

In one smooth motion, she handed the laptop and coat to Mac. She stood blocking the outside door, and smiled at the approaching guy. She took a step toward him, and Mac took that distraction to slip out through the door.

"Hi Dave. Merry Christmas." Jenna flashed a quick smile.

"You've still got on your coat. Where are you going? We've got a group up in four-o-two. Christine put all the pictures of our retreat last summer on a DVD. Come on up and check it out."

"I left my purse in the car. I'd better go grab it." She said.

"Okay, see you in a few."

She nodded and stepped outside. She felt the chill of the cold night, wrapped her coat tighter, and ran for Mac's car. Mac fired the engine, as she jumped in. He left the parking lot and eased east on the adjacent street. "All in all, this mission went quite well. Better than I had anticipated." He laughed.

"A few glitches, but we managed to make it out of there with Al's stuff." She settled back into the seat and pulled on her seat belt. "Are you sure you want to drive? If you don't, drive over to MacDonald's, we can switch drivers. If not, drive one more block south and then turn left going east. That will take us to I-80."

*****

"No, I'm feeling better. However, I'm serious. You'd make a good FBI agent. You think fast and lie believably." He chuckled.

"It comes from long experience." She shrugged.

"Claire told me something of how you two became friends." He said.

"My whole dark history, I suppose?" She dropped her voice.

"We all have those dark places in our lives. If we're smart; we learn from them. You seem to have done that."

"I've worked so hard to build a normal life, but sometimes I really miss my sister. I wish I could just call her and meet her for lunch; the way normal sisters do." She sighed. "I still have those empty places in my heart. Claire and Suzanne really helped me, and my adult life is fairly fulfilling."

"Suzy would spice up anyone's life. Now you have met Al. He seems like a nice guy, and he definitely has an attraction for you." Mac said.

"He's just mighty grateful I rescued him, and provided him with food and shelter on a cold snowy night. Sounds like the first line of a Snoopy novel." She laughed.

"Never –the- less, I think there's more to him than just gratitude. I'll find out more about him, once I arrive in London."

"Is that the plan? You're going to travel overseas and deliver the disc?" Jenna asked.

"Yes, I thought about which end of the transaction, and where the security breach really is. Alistair's London side, or the inventors of the batteries side. These young guys from BYU, they could be pretty naive. While I've been living in St. George, I've found Mormons sometimes trust people, when they really shouldn't."

"Any incident in particular/" She asked.

"One of my cases involved an older woman of that population. She was being scammed by a member of her congregation. She trusted him, mainly because he came to church every Sunday. It was her son, who called me, and asked us to investigate the man. We managed to save her from handing over her life savings to him. Over a million dollars."

"We heard of people like that in California from time to time. I suppose it's pretty common, especially now since the economy was down and now then up. But now even though things are now better. Some people have never regained their resources." She said. "One thing about the members of the FLDS, they are anything but trusting. Paranoia is the norm. They work to keep their members in and others out."

"Not a healthy way to live. Mac mused. "By taking away their freedom, in this case the girls and women, while the leaders work to take control of half the population, and it impedes the whole colony."

"You're correct on that one. It's more than just interesting, that in nearly every culture, religion is at the root of the control. Can't let us women have our freedom, that would take away the dominance of the men." Her laugh was bitter.

"I for one, believe in equality for women, let them learn and develop as much as they can. When a truly free woman comes to a man and wants to bond with him, that is an indication that she views him as also free. If it were not for Claire, you wouldn't be talking to me now."

"I know, I learned how she and Suzy rescued you from the morgue." Jenna said.

"She repeated the act. And she took it upon herself to gain as much information about the human body, its defenses and weaknesses as she could. She used her knowledge to defeat the enemy. That's all I can say, because the rest is classified."

"Well, all I can say is, Wow!"

Chapter Nine

When they reached the cottage, the only light inside came from the little Christmas tree.

As Mac and Jenna walked into the kitchen Mac grinned. "It's late, and this is Claire's way of telling us to go to bed."

At the mention of her name, Claire came down the stairs, kissed Mac and turned to Jenna. "I put Alistair in your bed. I gave him a pain pill, and he fell asleep pretty quickly. Your nightgown and robe are in the bathroom, and I pulled out the sofa bed for you, unless you want to climb in with Al."

Jenna tilted her head and answered with a slight shake of her head. "No, I'll sleep on the bed couch. We need to be out of here by noon tomorrow. Perhaps you can get Al in the shower tomorrow morning, Mac. He's getting a little 'ripe'."

"Before you go into the bathroom, Jenna, there's milk and cookies." Claire waved in the direction of the kitchen. She hooked her arm into Mac's arm. "Come husband, let's go to bed."

Jenna went into the kitchen for the offered dessert. When she bit into a cookie, she found it unique and marvelous, and wondered where Claire had bought them. She'd ask her in the morning.

Later that night Jenna lay in her cocoon of blankets and stared at the little tree. *Why is that I finally meet a great guy, and his home is seven thousand miles away?* Why couldn't he be an American? Already they had a connection. It was almost electric; a zing running through her bloodstream. Tomorrow he would leave, and she would clean out the cottage, and go back to her life and her job in Salt Lake. *Isn't that what you want, girl? No connection to a man who wants to tell you what to do?*

But Al had chipped through the well-hidden emptiness in her soul. She couldn't stop the tears from seeping down the side of the pillow and onto the mattress. The pillow that held his marvelous aroma.

Jenna awoke to the delicious aroma of dripping coffee. It was definitely time to get up and start breakfast. She hurried to the bathroom and slipped on her clothes. She found Mac pouring that first mug of coffee.

Jenna poured a mug for herself and opened the refrigerator. But she could nothing more than stare at its contents. This was their last morning all together, and she felt the tears gathering behind her eyelids. A gentle hand touched her shoulder.

"Are you finding any treasures or secrets in that fridge we could use?" Claire said.

"I'll pull out everything and you can take a look." Jenna began emptying the fridge and putting it on the counter.

"Hmmm, we have five eggs, some bacon, part of a loaf of apple bread. Plus part of a roast chicken, rolls, orange juice and a package of cheese.. "Let's use the eggs, apple bread, and bacon for breakfast, and use the rest for lunch on the road. Claire put on the teakettle, and reached for a box of herbal teas.

"Don't you want coffee?" Jenna asked.

"I'm off the 'hard' stuff for the duration." Claire glanced at Jenna and smiled.

For a moment, Jenna studied Claire's face, and took a long look at her body wrapped up in a robe. "You're pregnant? Great! When, I mean when' is it due?"

"April fifteenth, income Tax Day." She reached for Jenna and hugged her.

"I'm amazed, because you hide it so well. I get to be a second-hand aunt. Are you feeling okay?"

"I'm fine, and have passed the morning sickness, and the sleepiness days. But now when I drive long distances, I have to stop, and check out the cleanliness of all the restrooms across the west. Other than that, I feel pretty good."

"Now, back to breakfast. While we cook, fix up lunch snacks, and generally clean up the kitchen. As we accomplish this chore, the guys can clean up themselves, and afterward we can have the bathrooms to ourselves."

"Sounds like a plan." Jenna reached for a large pie plate, and began to crack eggs in it'. The basic ingredient for French toast.

*****

Alistair sat back and stretched his good arm. "I thought I was the recipient of food from the greatest cook in the world. Now I must praise the attributes of both the females in this cottage. Thank you both for a gourmet breakfast."

"We thank you. We'll let you know when we open our waffle house." Claire laughed. "Now, are the bathrooms free for the two chefs extraordinaire? We need time to clean up, and get beautiful."

"The steamy bathrooms with all wet towels on the floor are all yours." Mac quipped.

"Thanks a bunch, husband. I thought I'd trained you better than that." Claire said.

"Come on, we've been married less than a year. I read somewhere it takes at least five years for the complete course of husband taming. What I want to know is? Do I get a diploma?" Mac wiggled his eyebrows and grinned.

"We'll discuss that later." Claire said, and with her nose in the air, she left the kitchen.

It was after ten a.m. when the last of the luggage, food sacks and heavy coats were loaded into the two automobiles. Jenna and Mac's belongings were loaded in her Lexus, and Alistair's and Claire's things went into the Subaru. The sheets and towels had been gathered up and bundled for the cleaning crew, and the little Christmas tree was stripped bare of its trimmings.

They sat around the kitchen table and Mac laid out the plans for the next few days. "I snagged a seat on Delta to JFK, and have a connecting flight into Heathrow. Depending on the weather, I should arrive in jolly old England, tomorrow around twelve thirty P.M. their local time. My plan is to call for an appointment to see Rutledge, the CEO of World Wide, either that afternoon, or first thing the next morning. Jenna if you will be so kind to drop me off at the Salt Lake Terminal?"

"Of course." She nodded.

"Claire and Alistair will drive back to our house in the St. George area this afternoon. Tomorrow, she will drive him to Las Vegas and he will board an American Airlines plane bound for Houston. Alistair, you'll connect with another flight for Manchester, England. Take a train to the town where your apartment is located, and I'll call you with further instructions. We've already discussed this. If for any reason, it is better for you to stay in St. George for another day or two, I'll call and let you know, and why."

"Jenna, you will check into your hotel room and stay there. Don't go out unless you are with other people. Tuesday morning you go to your meeting and presentation. I have called the Cottonwood Police Department, and they want pictures of your car. They will meet you in the parking garage, when you arrive at your hotel, this afternoon. Okay gang, let's hit the road."

As Jenna loaded that last small bag in her car, Alistair came close to her. "It's been a terrible and wonderful Christmas with you. I still don't know how to thank you for saving me. I have no idea what the near future will bring, but we'll connect again, I'm sure of it." He took her face in his hands and kissed her with sweetness and passion. For a moment he rested his head on her forehead, squeezed her hand, but turned to slide into Claire's car. She and Mac had their arms around each other, kissing and laughing at some private married joke.

"We'll all see each other again, and I'll put good money on it being soon." Mac waved and slid into the passenger seat of Jenna's car and snapped on the seat belt.

Salt Lake International was crowded and bustling. Naturally, the 26th of December was a heavily traveled day, as would be the rest of

Christmas week. Jenna managed to pull her car in close to the curb, and the baggage handler. She handed Mac a sack lunch. "You won't get any food on the domestic flight. Claire and I didn't want you to go hungry."

He opened his briefcase and slid in the sandwich, apple and cookies. "Thanks Jenna. This will at least get me to the JFK."

"What time does your flight leave for London?" She asked.

Eight-fifteen P.M. A red eye. I've learned to sleep whenever and wherever I can. This may turn out to be a real interesting case. I have a gut feeling it will. Thanks for calling Claire and allowing us to get involved."

"Thank you for driving 300 plus miles on Christmas Day. Claire would make a great doctor. I could tell Al felt much better this morning. Good luck." She hugged him.

He turned, grinned, and flashed those emerald green eyes at her. "I love the puzzle this caper presents. You be wary, and take it easy. We'll see you soon." He turned and strolled into the terminal, disappearing with the throng of travelers.

CHAPTER TEN

Jenna left the air terminal, picked up the freeway for the short drive to the Sheraton, located in down town Salt Lake.

When she dragged her belongings into her assigned room, her cell phone was jangling a Christmas tune. "Hello?"

She heard. "Ms. Barlow, this is the Cottonwood Police. Could you come down to the parking garage?"

"Yes, to whom am I speaking?"

"Detective Brussard. You can't miss me; I'm gray haired and quite tall."

Tall was an understatement. Det. Brussard was about six foot six. He and his partner, Det. Franz were as opposite as a summer day, was from a winter storm in progress. While Brussard was tall and lean, Franz stood about five-eight, and had a heavy build. They had already located her damaged car.

Det Franz was taking pictures of the bullet's damage. She watched as Brussard dug out the shell from the back hatch. They also carefully examined the interior. Franz turned to her. "We need a statement, as to how and where the shots were fired at this automobile."

Jenna stood with her arms tightly wrapped around body. It was cold and drafty in the garage. She should have worn her coat.

Brussard spoke up. "There's a coffee shop in the hotel area. Let's go in there and have a drink, and you can tell us what transpired. No need for you to come into our offices eight miles away."

They found a rear booth and sat down. While Jenna told her story, the detective typed into an electronic notebook. Jenna finished, and sipped her coffee. She glossed over the injury that Alistair had received.

"Now Ms. Barlow, just so we understand what happened on December twenty-third just after nine p.m. Mr. Powell jumped into your car, on the fifth level of the parking garage. How soon after he entered was the first shot fired at your car?"

Jenna closed her eyes, and tried for mental picture of the scene. "Perhaps twenty to thirty seconds."

"And you say you heard two 'pops' thinking they were gun shots before he entered?"

"Yes, two."

"Do you know where Mr. Powell is now?"

"Yes, he's with my friend Claire MacCandlass."

"Ms. MacCandlass is married to Dexter MacCandlass? Why did she take him with her, rather than he staying with you?" Brussard asked. His was voice even, but all business.

"Her husband decided that Alistair would be safer out of the area, and she has a business to run. She must open it tomorrow." (a white lie.)

"How long will you be staying in this hotel?" Franz asked.

"Two nights. Tonight and tomorrow night. Then I am moving into a condo I have rented. It's being painted now." Jenna answered, and wrote down the address of where she would live.

"Thank you, Ms. Barlow. If we have any more questions, we'll contact you." The two of them shook her hand, slid from the booth and walked out of the coffee shop. Brussard, tall with a shock of graying hair, maybe 50, and Franz, younger, overweight, with closely cropped hair, hinting of blond. *Why didn't they ask where Mac was? Possibly because he has already contacted them.*

From the cottage in Coleville, Claire had driven to Park City, from there to Heber and on down State Route 40 to Orem, Utah. There she and picked up I-15 going south. Alistair was amazed at the snowy mountain vista, and was a little sad when they suddenly were driving on a freeway leaving the snow-covered mountains behind.

Claire, driving at freeway speed, took them through a wide valley with less snow accumulation. The suburbs of Provo gave way to small towns, and the mountain range to the west all but disappeared.

"This state of Utah has a varied topographical area." He commented.

"You ain't seen nuthin yet." She teased. "Wait until we get into the desert area and down into St. George."

"How much farther to your home city?" He asked."

"We'll be coming into Nephi in another few miles. From there, Rawley is about two- hundred twenty miles. We'll make a bathroom stop in Nephi. I'll take you into a convenience store. You'll be able to buy coffee, or a soda, but no tea, and tacky souvenirs if you like."

The stop was quick, and he decided not to buy any American trinkets. To go along with his soda, he grabbed the lunch sack the girls had packed for each car. In it he found small chicken sandwiches made with the rolls, apples and a cookie. He passed a sandwich to Claire, and soon they had finished off the contents of the sack.

The next town of any consequence was called Fillmore. She began to tell him the history of this town. "At one time this place was the capital of Deseret. It's named after Millard Fillmore who was a president of the United States.at that time. He was hostile to the Mormons because of polygamy. I'm not sure whether they named this county and town to appease him, or perhaps insult him."

"What is Deseret?" He asked.

"It was the name of the Utah territory where the Mormons first settled, and was much larger than it is now. But when statehood came, and The U. S. Congress whittled it down to the size the present Utah is now. They had to give up quite a bit of territory. Maybe we can find a map of the original Deseret on the internet."

The next town they came to was called Beaver. "Don't ask me how this place got its name. Time for another bathroom stop." They stopped at a truckers' convenience store, and bought candy bars and ice cream. There they also bought gasoline.

They dropped in elevation into a town called Cedar City. "In the summer we have a Shakespeare Festival here. It's very popular. It goes from June through September."

Alistair had felt the deep cold of Beaver, and even Cedar City showed evidence of a recent snow storm. From this town they drove down, and down dropping in elevation from 5700 feet above sea level to the desert, the mesas and buttes of St. George. The sandstone rock showed shades red, orange to yellow, and he recognized it to be different rock formation from that of Cedar City.

When they drove into areas below 3000 feet elevation, they drove into the main area of St. George. Claire took a street through the main part of town and turned onto a road going west. They passed subdivisions of newer houses, but soon the new homes gave way to older places, with larger tracts of land.

Abruptly, she slowed and turned right into a gravel drive on the west side of a white clapboard house. It had black shutters, a dark roof, and a wide porch spanning the front of the place. She parked the car not far from a large green structure that could be a barn. She walked around the car and opened a side door into the house with glass window near the top of the door.

He decided it could be a kitchen door. Alistair, stiff and in some pain, stretched, managed to pick up his valise, and carry it into another proper kitchen. This one was larger than the cottage kitchen, but its design was similar. The food preparation area was to the south side of the room. Whereas the eating area, again was nestled in a bay window facing north. The kitchen was decorated in the same colors as the outside of the house, black and white.

Claire made another trip out to the car, bringing in more belongings, so Alistair followed her out to help empty the car. The first thing he noticed was the temperature. It was almost balmy.

"It's much warmer here." He commented.

"Yes, lower elevation, and further south, but we still have to heat the house in the winter. Come in, I'll show you to your room, and turn up the thermostat." She walked out of the kitchen, into the front hall to a stairway leading up. The stairs went to an attic type second story, or in some houses called a story and a half. She led him down a short hall to a room on the north.

"This is your room, and you have your own private bathroom.

Unpack and get comfortable. In a bit, I'll make us some supper."

At that moment he heard her cell phone ring, and she turned and ran down the stairs. The ringing stopped, and he listened to her voice, but could not understand what she said.

He checked his watch: five-fifty P.M. He'd like to call Jenna. Since he had lost his cell phone, perhaps he could use the land line in the house. He turned and surveyed the room, not large, but functional. It had a masculine feel to it. A desk and chair were by a west facing window. A queen-sized bed was against the north wall, with three square windows high on the wall above. There was a short cotton drape on the windows, in a navy, gray and white pattern. The same fabric draped the west sash window. He pulled it back and could see Claire's car below.

The peak of the ceiling was high, perhaps thirteen or fourteen feet. A ceiling fan and light unit had been installed in the exact middle of the room. As he studied the room, he understood its design. It was built to be comfortable in hot weather. Opening the windows would give cross ventilation, and the ceiling fan would help to cool the room. A door closer to the wall led to a bathroom, with two sinks, toilet and shower. Beyond that was a small walk-in closet. It was a short L shape, and there were built in shelves and a long hanging rod. The closet was nearly empty, and he began emptying his valise and hanging up his clothes.

Alistair liked this house. It had a friendly, well used feel. He supposed architecturally it would classify as an American farm house, or perhaps they could call it a bungalow. He liked the red spires of rock in this area. To him they epitomized the fresh, Western American lifestyle.

He eyed the bed, and sat down on it. It seemed to be comfortable. So, he folded down the navy-blue spread, kicked off his shoes, turned off the overhead light, and lay down. Exhaustion had caught up, and he closed his eyes.

Chapter Eleven

Sometime later Alistair heard Claire calling his name. He sat up, disoriented. Where was he? Where was Jenna? He looked around the nearly dark bedroom. Now he remembered that he was upstairs in Claire and Mac's house.

"Alistair, did you hear me. I have supper ready."

"Sorry, coming. I fell asleep." He eased down the stairs and walked into the bright, warm kitchen. He smelled some delicious soup, and sat down where she directed. She went to the oven and took out an open-faced sandwich with cheese on top.

Claire cut the bread in two uneven pieces, handing him the larger slice on a white, china plate. She ladled hot beef soup into bowls, and set them on the table. As the aroma of the soup teased his nose, his stomach rumbled. He took a spoonful and he was not disappointed. "This is marvelous." He smiled and took another sip.

"I don't know about marvelous, but it is nourishing." She began eating. They were both quiet, enjoying the food for a few minutes. "Mac called. He talked to me all the way until he boarded the plane. But the call ended, because they made him shut down his phone. He has called the Salt Lake FBI, and they will probably want to talk to you. They already have plans to visit the young inventors of the batteries, and check on their contacts. So maybe you'll need to hang out with me another day or so."

"I would be most delighted to stay here. Also, I am curious about this area of the country. Its grandeur is breathtaking."

"You might have second thoughts about this town, if you came for a visit in July."

"Is it really that hot here in the summer?" He asked.

"Oh yes, It's over 100 degrees each day for most of the summer season. I'll give you a tour tomorrow. I must open the animal clinic at eight a.m. but I could come back late morning and take you for a drive."

"That would be super." He continued to eat. A minute or two later the phone rang.

Claire pulled the cell phone from her pocket. "Hello?" She listened, and she frowned, as she held the phone out. "Alistair, it's for you."

*****

"Alistair, this is Jenna."

"Jenna, so nice to speak with you. Did you reach your hotel?"

"Yes, I'm here. I want to warn you. The Cottonwood police examined my car for bullet hole damage, and interviewed me. I told them basically what happened, and where you are."

"Will they want to speak with me, too?" He asked.

"I tried to vague about your injuries, but I do think someone will want to interview you. It may be that it will be the local St. George police, or the Cottonwood guys will drive down to talk to you."

"When they find me, I'll tell them my version of what happened in the parking garage" He tried for a laugh. "I'm sorry my action of seeking refuge in your car has involved into this. Could we call it, a messy incident?"

"But I *am* involved. It was my choice to help you. We'll deal with the consequences. I'm certainly glad I thought to bring in Mac and Claire. Besides, I enjoyed having you has a guest at Christmas."

"And I so enjoyed being with you. It will be one Christmas I won't soon forget, but I want you to be careful. Those, thugs, as you labeled them, may still be active. You are their only source to finding me."

"Mac warned me, too. Not to go out without other people. Someone's at the door."

He heard her walk to the door and open it. She spoke to the guest. Then she said. "Alistair, I'll get back to you in a couple of hours.

I'm going out for dinner. Take care. Bye."

Alistair sat back down and sipped his tea. "I suppose we just wait and see which group of lawmen locate me first."

"Lawmen, listen to you. You've been watching too much American TV. If you want to indulge in TV watching a little more, there's a television in the room across the hall. It was a bedroom, but I made it into a den- office area. Go relax. I'm going up to unpack, and do some laundry." Claire set the dishes in the sink, and he heard her climb the stairs.

December 27th, Eleven a.m., London

Mac moved along with the throng of passengers deplaning at Heathrow. He waited in line at the customs window, but was waved through, when he showed the man his FBI Identification. Next was a ride down an escalator ride to baggage claim.

Once he picked up his luggage, he sat down and called World Wide Electronics, and asked to speak with Howard Rutledge.

Finally, he was put though and heard. "Rutledge here. I don't remember a Mr. MacCandlass."

"If I can speak to you privately, I'll explain, who I am and who I represent." Mac said.

"I'm a busy man, and several appointments. I really don't think-
- - - - - -?"

"It's concerning Alistair Powell." Mac said.

"Alistair? Is he with you? Do you know where he is?" Rutledge's voice rose in concern, along with a niggle of fear? Mac could hear the man's breathing quicken.

"If we can meet in person, I will be able to explain a few things to you about what happened to Alistair." Mac pushed.

"Of course. Are you close by the Ridge building? We're on the fifth floor. I'd be pleased to see you around, say two o'clock?"

"Give me the address." Mac asked.

Rutledge rattled it off. "Thank you for calling." He clicked off.

Mac stood, and then had to drag his suitcase into an elevator. From the third floor, he moved to a van service. A few minutes later, he boarded a van taking him into downtown London. He exited his ride and walked a half block to the *White Horse* Hotel.

After checking in, he took his laptop and headed in the direction of the Ridge building. He passed a little shop with the name: *Millie's Tea Room*. His stomach was still functioning on St. George, Mountain Time, and he felt fuzzy headed from lack of sleep. The wind had picked up and a smattering of cold rain began to fall. Although the place seemed crowded, he opted to go in, at least to get into a place, and out of the raw chill.

His first impression of the shop was delicious warmth, and the aroma of freshly baked products. All this mingled with food simmering and coffee perking. He waited for a few minutes, until it came to be his turn at the tall counter. A plump girl, wearing a large white apron asked for his order.

"Would you like to eat it here, or are you ordering it take-a-way?" Beads of sweat dampened her dark hair.

"I'd prefer to eat here, if possible." He answered.

"Be a moment, then." She answered.

He looked around the small room. All five round tables were occupied. Suddenly the four people sitting at the corner table got up to leave. The counter girl came out with a tray, and cleaned off the table.

"Sir, you may sit here." She motioned to the table she had just cleared.

He walked to a table which had a marble finish and white metal chairs. He set his laptop on it, and faced the window. The girl brought over his buttered crescent and a large, china mug of coffee. He sipped and watched as the once crowded shop began to empty. Glancing at his watch, he read twelve fifty-five P.M. These people most likely were returning to work.

A few minutes later a large, middle-aged woman came to his table. "I heard you place your order. A yank are ye?" As he looked up at her. the best way to describe her would be robust. "I'm Millie, by the way." Her salt and pepper hair was pulled up in a bun, and slightly curling tendrils had escaped. They hung by her temples, and the back of her neck.

"Yes, recently off a plane landing at Heathrow?" He couldn't help but smile at the woman.

"Took the 'red eye' from California, did ye?"

"Close enough, Utah." He laughed.

"Well now. That kind of fare you're eatin' won't keep a big man like yerself movin' about for long. You need some of Millie's, beef and dumplin' soup. She turned and called out. "Kristy, bring the man a bowl."

As he ladled a large spoonful into his mouth, he couldn't help but sigh. The soup was hot, thick and delicious.

Millie stood gazing at him from behind the counter. "You have business close by?"

"Yes, an appointment at the Ridge building."

Mac decided to point the conversation in another direction. "Do you get many customers in from that building?"

"Yes, many secretaries, such as that."

"Do you ever remember an Alistair Powell? He's a tall man, about my height, medium brown hair, and eyes. Probably close to my age."

"Kristy, do you remember an Alistair from the charging slips?"

"Yes, he didn't work over at the building, but at the manufacturing plant, south. He'd come in for a meeting, and such. Nice fellow, polite. I believe he was chief engineer at the plant. Mister, are you from someplace in the States' where it snows?"

"We live, my wife and I, in the very southern part of the state of Utah. It's a desert region, but once in a while it will snow." He smiled at the girl.

"We had snow here last week, and last year it snowed a record."

Millie said. "Some say it's global warming, hah!" She put her elbow in top of the counter, and stared at him. "Where did you get that copper penny hair, and fair skin, Gingerboy?"

"Gingerboy?" His eyes narrowed. "My lineage is Scottish." He rubbed a hand over his head.

She came around the counter and gazed down at him. "Ah yes, that's what I said. A boy with red hair and green eyes. I see those emerald eyes are from here. I can."

"Yep, my mother had red hair." He glanced at his watch, and then walked to the counter and studied the menu board. "How much for the soup?" He asked.

"No charge. Come in for a good English breakfast tomorrow." Millie held the door open for him as he ran out into the rain.

CHAPTER TWELVE

World Wide Electronics, Limited took up most of the fifth floorof the Ridge Building. The set up reminded Mac of any number of corporate offices he had visited in the U.S. He went directly to Rutledge's office and announced himself. A few moments later he was ushered into a large, lush office with all the accoutrements of an executive suite. It was expansive, with 'acres' of dark blue-gray carpet. Tall windows looking out over the city were the backdrop for a large cherry wood desk and credenza.

"Come in, come in." Rutledge waved, and allowed Mac to stride over to his desk, before he stood up. He was a little man, and had to reach over the desk to shake hands with his guest. He wore an expensive designer suit, and a shirt that probably cost more than Claire spent in a week on groceries. But underneath those clothes was a soft body, overly fond of rich food and drink.

"Sit down, sit down. When did you arrive in London?" He took a deep breath and sat back in his fine leather chair. Now, MacCandlass, you're from America, right?"

"Yes, I'm from the States." Mac answered.

"So did you come here representing Alistair Powell?" Rutledge looked intently at Mac.

"A friend of a friend called me and informed me about Alistair. He had been attacked and shot."

"Shot! Oh dear, how serious is it?"

"He's under medical care, but I must inform you. Please understand, he's being pursued by foreign nationals. He has gone to ground." Mac answered with a unemotional gaze.

"He was sent to the Western part of the United States as a representative of our company, to investigate a new product. One that we could possibly use in some of our products we manufacture.

I heard from him that he was going to witness a demonstration. We've had no communication after that from him." Rutledge leaned forward. "Do you know if he has in his possession a flash drive or disc of the product given to him by that American company?"

Mac gave him a questioning gaze. "Flash drive? or disc?" Mac shook his head. "I was hired to keep him safe, and find a medic for him. So, on that note, Alistair mentioned that your company would be able to take care of my expenses." Mac produced a sheet of paper from his briefcase, an itemized list of his expenses for the three days he had been involved with Alistair.

With shaking hands Rutledge glanced at the paper. "This is for nearly five thousand pounds?"

"Yes, air fare. a hotel, the safe house for Alistair, and of course medical care. It will probably be more before this case come to a conclusion.

Those were foreign nationals who tried to kill Alistair. I've been hired to investigate all the possibilities. I'm sure you would want a satisfactory solution to this crime, wouldn't you?"

"Yes, yes, of course." Rutledge picked up the phone and called in his secretary. "Alistair's safety is utmost." Ms. Thorne came into the office. A middle-aged woman, properly dressed in a gray suit, her graying hair pulled up in a strict bun.

"Please take this to Greenlee and have him cut a check for Mr. MacCandlass. Make a copy of this invoice for our files." Rutledge sat down heavily.

"Yes sir." She stared down a Mac for a long moment. She frowned, but then turned and left.

"You live in the State of Utah?" Rutledge made nervous taps on this desk pad with a pencil.

"Yes, part of the time. I also work out of Las Vegas. I'm a liaison for the FBI."

Rutledge sat back in his chair as if to put distance between Mac and himself. "You were with the FBI? What sorts of cases have you come across in your work?"

"Mostly chasing down and capturing foreign nationals hostile to the U. S." Mac answered his face stern.

"Oh my, I'm sure that it was very interesting work, and you must have been quite good at it." Mac watched the man begin to perspire, and loosen his shirt collar.

"Yes, I and several others were quite involved." Mac gave him a deadpan look.

The door opened and Ms. Thorne walked in carrying a large white envelope. She set it on Rutledge's desk and stood back. "Is there anything else? Mr. Rutledge?'

"No, resume your normal duties." The woman turned on her heel and left.

On cue Mac stood, and picked up his briefcase. "I've other individuals to contact so I'll be leaving now."

"Mr. MacCandlass, if you know where the disc or information that Alistair had in his possession is located, I'd appreciate you bringing it to me. It does belong to World Wide Electronics."

"It may still be in the parking garage where Alistair was chased, shot and lost his cell phone. He was running for his life, and possibly dropped it. Yesterday, the local police were searching for it, or anything else having to do with the crime committed against Alistair." Mac stood and walked to the double doors of the office and turned. "Good day, Mr. Rutledge."

December 27th, eight a.m.
Mountain Standard Time, Salt Lake City

At a little after eight A. M. that morning, Jenna drove her car into the parking garage, and chose a slot on the fifth level. Her plan was to set up her power point presentation before any of the Alta-Angeles employees arrived. The level was nearly deserted. As she punched the button on the small elevator, all she could see was a bakery truck parked close to the elevator. They must be bringing in breakfast.

Making her way to the elevator had been awkward, because she not only carried her laptop, briefcase, but also an art folder. Just as she boarded the elevator, two Asian men pushed their way in. The man closer to Jenna grabbed her arm in a tight grip and said, in accented English. "Ms. Barlow, you need to come with us."

She had backed into the corner, but could reach the elevator panel. With her other hand she hit the open-door button. The man holding her growled, tightened his hold, and twisted her arm painfully. The other man asked something in a language she did not understand.

"Let go of me!" She screamed in fear but also anger. Suddenly, the closing door was pushed open, and two more men pushed into the small car. Both were wearing tan top coats, and one shoved a weapon into the side of the man holding Jenna. "Not a good idea to harass Ms. Barlow on her way to work."

Immediately the second Asian, kicked at the second tan coated man. That man turned, and with a swift martial arts attack, pinned the Asian man to the floor. The elevator went up one level, and the doors slid open. A third man in a tan coat dragged away the man holding Jenna, threw him to the floor, and hand cuffed him. The first man in the tan coat had the Asian man pinned to the floor by his foot. He dragged him up and hand cuffed him, too.

Jenna sagged against the wall of the elevator. "Are you guys FBI?"

"Yes ma'am." The third man took out his identification for her to examine. He turned to the two others. "Take them to the van. I'll escort Ms. Barlow to her offices." He came into the elevator, and turned to Jenna. "Choose your floor, ma'am."

Once they reached her office floor, he helped her carry her belongings into the board room, where she was to do her presentation. "Did MacCandlass call you guys? Whoever alerted you three, I certainly want to thank you."

"Mac called us, yes. We also were asked to be on alert by the Cottonwood Police. This incident with you and Mr. Powell, we suspect, has international ramifications. We had to witness a crime in progress so we could charge these NK's. Trying to kidnap you will do. Sorry if that guy hurt you."

She put her hand to her heart. "I can't say I enjoyed being roughed up by those thugs, but if I can be any more help, just let me know. Thank you again for your assistance. Oh, one more question, were you guys in the bakery van?"

The man's lips twitched. "It works well as a cover vehicle. Thank you, Ms. Barlow." He nodded to her, and walked to the elevator.

The adrenalin rush left her, and she began to shake. She pulled her purse from inside her laptop bag and made for the women's restroom.

Her face was white, and her knees didn't want to support her. She soaked a paper towel and mopped her neck, and cheeks. Her arm hurt where the thug had dug in. Taking off her gray jacket and rolling up the sleeves of her pink blouse she found marks on her arm. One had broken the skin. "Dammit, that jerk has long fingernails. Where is he from, the Ding Bat dynasty?!" She yelled at the mirror, but scrubbed her arm with soap and blotted it dry. Once she had repaired her makeup she felt better, and went back to the conference room.

A few minutes later, actual caterers came in to set up a breakfast, and she grabbed a cup of coffee. As she sipped the brew, she forced her mind to go to the chore of setting up her presentation. Soon she was ready.

Three-thirty p.m. December 27th, London

As Mac walked the three streets to the *White Horse Hotel*, he was glad he had thought to bring his zip-lined trench coat. The rain had stopped, but the wind had not. If he stayed here much longer, he would have to buy a hat.

His room, though small, was heated with a radiator, and the bed was high and comfortable. He pulled off his coat, jacket and flopped on the bed. He needed to contact the local authorities, but would they listen to him? Then he had an idea, grabbed his cell phone, and called his ex-partner in Las Vegas.

"Federal Bureau of Investigation, Las Vegas Office, Forester speaking."

"Dan this is Mac, how goes it in sunny Las Vegas?"

"Mac, I haven't heard from you for what, six months? Where are *you,*, and what are you up to, now?"

"I'm in London on a case. I wondered if you still had contact with that Scotland Yard guy you worked with a few years ago?"

"Okay, but before I give you this guy's name, I want to know what's going on? Every time you start on a simple caper, you get in over your head."

"This one began with a call from an old friend of Claire's" Mac went on to explain how he and Claire got involved. Which now looks like something big and international" He said.

"This Alistair Powell, individual is with Claire, as we speak? I'd like to take a look at that disc." Dan Forester said. He was silent for a moment. "Did you get the Salt Lake agents involved?"

"I called them, mainly because I was concerned for Jenna's safety. Also, I just had an interview with Alistair's boss, Rutledge. He's dirty, I can smell it." Mac said.

"Yeah, you'd better inform Scotland Yard. Hang on. I've got him on my computer." He left the phone for a few minutes. "Okay, His name is Hugh McIntire. He's sharp, good to work with. I'll give you his private exchange, and cell phone number." Dan rattled off both numbers. "Look, I'm going to talk to Strickland. I'll bet he'll give me the go ahead to interview Powell. Keep me in the loop. Call me later."

Dan can't resist an interesting case. He's got the blood hound mentality. Mac picked up his cell phone and dialed the local London exchange.

CHAPTER THIRTEEN

"McIntire, here." The man answered.

"I'm Dexter MacCandlass, Dan Forester was my partner. I'm here in London, and have some information for you. Would you be kind enough to meet with me?"

"I'm listening, Mr. MacCandlass. Who on our side of the 'pond' does this concern?"

Quickly Mac explained who he represented, and why. Next, he told McIntire about his interview with Rutledge.

"Ah, our Mr. Rutledge. Yes, I'd be quite interested in meeting with you. When did you arrive in London?"

"This late morning. I talked to Rutledge less than an hour ago."

"Where are you staying?"

"*The White Horse Hotel.* Nice little hotel. Alistair recommended it." Mac answered.

"Tell you what. I've some work to complete. I'll review our files on Rutledge, and Powell. It's after three P.M. now. I'll meet you at the *Black Bull Tavern.* It's next to your hotel. Say about seven, this evening. Have the disc with you. Watch your back, because Rutledge sometimes employs a couple of goons. Describe to me who to look for?'

"I'm over six feet, one hundred ninety, and have red hair. What about you?"

"Close to six feet, and heavier than you. Dark hair, and I'm 48 and have the bags under my eyes to prove it. A least that's what my wife tells me. Meet you at seven P.M.."

This guy is going to be okay. Mac set the radio alarm clock for six forty- five P.M. pulled off his shoes, pulled up the duvet, and slept.

*****

About noon in St. George, the phone rang. "May I speak with Claire?"

"I must apologize; she's at her animal clinic. I can give you the number." Alistair said.

"Am I speaking with Alistair Powell?"

A tremor of fear went through Alistair, but he managed to answer with a calm voice. "Yes, this is he, speaking."

"Good, I'm Dan Forester. I was Mac's partner while he was with the FBI. Mac called me and explained your situation. I have permission from my boss to come and talk to you. My new partner, Angela Patton and I will be up there in two hours or so. I'll call Claire and let her know we're coming."

"You have permission for your director?'

"Yes. This attempt on your life is just part of a larger situation. Stay inside. Don't go anywhere. We'll meet you at Clair's house. Good bye."

"Good Bye to you." Alistair put down the phone. He realized that he had involved Jenna in a perilous situation, and he was seeing just the tip of the ice berg.

December 27th, Two P. M.
Mountain Standard Time, Provo

Once they reached the city of Provo, it took FBI agents Balfour and Higby nearly 20 minutes to find the old warehouse. It was west of the city and home to, *Ultimate Batteries Unlimited* : Jamison and Reacher owners. The building was old and as the agents soon found out, drafty on this late December afternoon. Since they had been in on the rescue of Jenna Barlow that morning they were to follow up with this next assignment.

They had called ahead and spoke to Jamison, so they were expected. They walked in and strolled around the high-ceilinged building and casually inspected the work tables and equipment. A stairway led to an upstairs office so they moved in that direction.

A tall, young man met them at the stairs. "Hi, I'm Paul Reacher, one of the owners. Come in. It's much warmer in here."

He was apparently dressed to work down in the chilly warehouse. He wore a turtle neck, a sweat shirt, and a jacket, boots and worn jeans. The office was warmer, and the agents were offered chairs by a scared wooden desk. Paul Reacher sat down behind it. Higby showed his ID badge to the young man.

"What is it you came to discuss with us?" He asked. His gaze was straight at them.

"We understand that you did a demonstration of your various batteries for a Mr. Alistair Powell from England? Is that correct?"

The steady eyes narrowed slightly, and little frown creased the young man's face. "That's correct. His company contacted us, because of information from an article about our company. It was in a computer magazine. Mr. Powell's company wanted a demonstration, and we invited him to come down here. He seemed very interested in our products. Is there a problem?"

"One more thing. You gave him a disc of the specs on your products. Is that correct?"

"Yes, some of the construction of our batteries cannot be publically shown, because we have patents pending. So, they were not on the disc. We did discuss with Mr. Powell about modifying our batteries to fit into their finished products. He seemed quite enthusiastic about the combined units."

"What time did Mr. Powell leave?" Agent Balfour asked.

"Hmmm, we had dinner brought in to this office. Tina picked it up. It was the four of us and Alistair. He left a little before eight P.M. He said something about Christmas shopping."

"Could you point out which of your employees were here when Mr. Powell watched the demonstration?" Higby asked.

Again, the slight frown creased his face. "Sure. John Jamison, was here, of course. And Markus Peal. Our part time guy Louis, left. And our computer geek, Tina Woo was here, because she picked up the food."

"Are they all here now?" Higby asked.

"Yes." The three of them walked out of the office and stood on the cat walk to the stairs.

"Hey guys. These investigators want to talk to all of us. Come up, please."

"I'll get us all some sodas. Call out your preferences." Balfour yelled. He started down the stairs and casually perused the work stations. Finally walking to a canned soda dispenser.

One by one they all came up and sat down around a big, old cherry wood table. The agent set down all the sodas in the middle of the table.

"Come on guys, time for a break, anyway." Paul said.

"We called all of you together, because we have a little problem. It may or may not involve people wanting knowledge of what you guys are constructing here. We'd like to talk to all of you." Agent Balfour said.

Tina looked over at John Jamison. "I really should stay with my circuitry work." She whined.

"Come on Tina. This won't take too long." John took her arm.

As she came into the room, Higby handed her a diet cola. "Enjoy, time for a break."

He sat down across from her and watched as she popped the tab and took a sip.

"Yes, thank you." She tried for a little smile, but he could see she was nervous.

Paul gathered up some blue prints, rolled them up and set them in a corner of the room. "Listen up guys, they want to explain why they're here in this meeting."

"We are with the FBI, investigating an attempted murder of Mr. Powell. It happened in Salt Lake at the Town Mall in the parking garage. We believe the perps wanted the disc your organization gave him. He planned on taking it back to the UK."

"That's terrible. Did you catch the criminals?" Markus asked.

"Yes, the local police did pick them up, but they were released yesterday on a technicality. However, we will still be investigating all aspects of the crime."

"Is he okay?" Paul said. "He seemed to be a really nice guy."

"We have medical help for him, and he has left the area." Balfour answered.

Tina's computer dinged softly. "I must go down and see if everything I called up has been downloaded." She jumped up and ran down the stairs to the main area.

"Well, that's all we can tell you about the case so far. We'll be in touch." Agent Balfour stood and shook hands with the others, while Higby eased around the table and carefully picked up Tina's can of soda, and dropped it into a plastic bag. The agents walked down the stairs to the entrance of the building, and waved goodbye to the employees.

Balfour buttoned his coat against the snow beginning to fall. "Our next stop should be a trip up to the University and the student admissions building."

Chapter Fourteen

Higby gave a swipe at the snow accumulating on the windshield. "We better get moving and return to Salt Lake, before this storm becomes a problem."

"I believe if you drive east, we'll find an entrance to the university complex. It begins east of the freeway." Balfour said. Soon they had arrived at the entrance to the university area, and Balfour went to the booth for a map.

With the map, they easily found the building where student services were located. Parking was no problem, because no classes were being held this December day: the 27th. Higby climbed out of the car and his stomach growled audibly. "I guess I'm hungry. We skipped lunch."

Balfour grinned. "Let's try to make this visit to student services a quick one."

At the information window they were helped by a young woman with the name on her badge: Wendy. When they asked for Tina Woo's student folder, she hesitated. "I don't know if I can let you see it." That information is confidential."

"We're from the FBI." Balfour flashed his identification. "May we speak with your supervisor?"

"Of course." She frowned and left the window.

A few minutes later an older, balding man came to the window. "I'm Mr. Hoffman. May I see your identification?"

Both agents showed Hoffman their ID.

"Here is Ms. Woo's admission materials and grading information. You will see from her grades, she is a exemplary student. There's a copy machine over there." He indicated to it. "It takes quarters. Why do you want to see her file?"

"We're just checking out several people in an investigation. Just routine." Higby said, and reached in his pocket for change. "Can you give me five dollars in quarters?"

Less than thirty minutes later they left the campus in a steady snow storm, and directions for the closest Arby's. "We'd better get this information back to our office. Our CSU people will want to take a look at the soda can."

In London, the rain had stopped, but the wind persisted, and the temperature had dropped. Mac hunched down into the collar of his top coat. He could understand why people living here, in busy London, England, wore wool jackets under their rain coats.

The Black Bull Tavern was noisy, dimly lighted, low ceilinged, and warm. For a moment he wondered if he should wait at the bar, or go left into the area where there were tables and food service. Instead, he stood watching people being seated at the tables. He began to scan the room for anyone resembling Chief McIntire.

A large hand clapped him on the shoulder, and he whirled around to face a big man with thinning black hair, and wide smile. "You must be MacCandlass."

"I am." Mac put out his hand, and McIntire gave it a vigorous shake.

McIntire called out to a man in a white apron. "Artie, you got a table for us?"

Artie glanced around, and waved them through to a table in the corner. "Two for dinner?"

McIntire nodded. "What the special tonight?"

"Grilled Turbo, potatoes, and salad, or roast turkey, stuffing, whipped potatoes, and green beans."

"What's yer pleasure, Mac?" Without waiting he said. "Bring us one of each. We'll fight it out when ya bring the food." McIntire grinned.

The table was constructed of some old wood, heavy, sturdy with a scarred top. The chairs had a barrel shape, and fit a man's frame comfortably. Artie brought a pot of tea and two mugs.

McIntire poured the tea and sat back. "So, you're a friend of Daniel Forester?"

"I was his partner for a few months." Mac answered.

"Now I remember the name. You were involved in the Las Vegas bombing case? What happened? Why did you resign?"

"An injury, and I met a girl, fell in love with her. We married, and now she's pregnant. I guess you could say I settled down." Mac gazed across the table at his new acquaintance.

McIntire took a small notebook from his inside jacket pocket. He wrote a name, and turned it for Mac to read. "This is the man you spoke with this afternoon?"

Mac glanced around the room and nodded.

"We'll be going back to my office after supper. "It wouldn't be wise to discuss it here."

"I understand." Mac nodded. Artie came with bowls of soup and a basket of bread. They both began to enjoy their supper.

When they both returned to McIntire's office, he went to a filing cabinet pulled a thick file for Mac to read.

After a few minutes Mac sat back, and met McIntire's eyes. "The reason why I came to London and called on Rutledge was, because he is Alistair Powell's boss." He then went on to explain the attack on Alistair, Jenna's involvement in the 'caper' and her connection to Claire.

"As you have read, our Mr. Rutledge has his 'fingers in several pies'. What attracted our attention to him is that he lives much too well on his eighty thousand quid a year income, would allow."

"What are your suspicions about Mr. Rutledge?" Mac asked.

"Dealing drugs to begin with. We think he has a very clever organization. We could pick him up on tax evasion tomorrow, but there are some bigger blokes involved. We're building a case against the North Korean connection, and this is a *new* one. They may be his supply route for the heroin his group peddles. I'm wondering which country or where in the Middle East they plan to sell the specs for the batteries. Or peddle the finished products all through that area of the world."

"But why attack Alistair Powell? Possibly they could just sell the plans to make the batteries, or the whole units? If his company planned to make and sell the computers and televisions legally, why steal it from Alistair?" Mac asked.

"Do you have a copy of the disc?" McIntire asked.

Mac reached into his jacket pocket and handed it to his host. He watched as McIntire found a flat manila envelope slipped in the disc and marked it. It also went into the Rutledge file.

"I believe that Rutledge owes the NK's, as you Americans would say, 'large'. Somehow, he has to repay them. What do they need? Money or product? I'll tell you what I would be buying if I were the leader of that miserable country, Food. They're starving over there."

Dan Forester and Angela Patton rang the doorbell of Claire's house at exactly two forty- five P. M. Claire turned to Alistair who was sitting at the kitchen table reading the local newspaper and sipping tea. "Don't get up until I call you. Then stroll into the living room, as if you were distracted from some important task."

"I understand. Hide the nervousness with a bit if irritation?"

"Right on, mate. Oops, wrong English-speaking country's idiom." She grinned but then turned down the hall to the front door.

"Dan, Angela, is it? Come in." Claire waved them in. "Sit down. I'll fetch Alistair."

Alistair sat down in the wing chairs by the front window. Just then a puff of wind blew against the window rattling the screen. Claire turned and glanced out. "Looks like a storm blowing in."

"You're correct on that one. We had a tail wind all the way in from Las Vegas." Dan said.

Alistair studied this Dan Forester. He was about his own height, but had a more athletic build. The man must spend time in the gymnasium, and probably at the gun range. Their general coloring was similar, brown hair, except that Dan's eyes were a gray and his own, a light brown.

Dan pulled out a tape recorder and set it on the coffee table next to his knees. "Taping a conversation is much more accurate."

Alistair nodded, but glanced at Claire.

"Now Alistair, state your name and address for the record."

"Alistair Powell, 922 Astor Street, South Londonderry, UK."

"Now, Mr. Powell, on the evening of December 23rd. this year. Please state what happened at approximately nine P.M. that evening, at the Town Mall in Salt Lake City." Dan said in a smooth interviewer's voice.

"I drove to the Mall, parked my car on the 5th level to do some shopping." He went on to tell about being chased and shot. Then he, in desperation jumped into Jenna's car.

"Mr. Powell, you had never before seen Ms. Barlow or her car?"

"No, I wanted to hide, get away, so I took a chance and jumped at her car." The interview went on, Alistair relating every detail.

"So, you say that the perps chased you and Ms. Barlow until she drove east to the thirty-ninth street onramp to I-80 East? What stopped them?"

"A mound of snow at the freeway entrance, and the Cottonwood Police."

"When did Ms. Barlow enlist the help of Mac and Claire MacCandlass?"

"On December 24th. Sometime in the afternoon."

"I'll take it from here, Dan." Claire interrupted.

Dan stopped the tape recorder.

"At this point I don't think Alistair can add anything more to your case." Claire said.

Dan frowned at Claire, but then he let out a heavy sigh. "Okay, your knowledge is important, too."

"Jenna called me on December 24th mid- afternoon. Mac and I arrived at the cottage near Coleville, Christmas Day, around six P.M. I examined Alistair's gunshot wound, redressed it and began antibiotic therapy."

"To your knowledge had Alistair seen a physician?" Dan asked.

"Yes, Jenna took him to the emergency room at the hospital on

39th Street, in Salt Lake County. However, I believe they left when the she spotted the perps carrying a weapon. I imagine she wanted to keep him from further harm. We still do not know who the preps are, who attacked him."

Dan shut down the tape recorder, and nodded finishing the interview. "Before we hit the road, Claire, how about some coffee?"

"Good old Dan." She touched his arm. "Sure, and I suppose you could choke down some pumpkin pie to go along with it."

"I won't turn down pie." For the first time, Alistair watched the man's face crease into a smile.

Dan drained the mug of the last drops of coffee. "Have you heard from Mac?"

"Not since he touched down in London, and that was early this morning. He told me he had an appointment with Rutledge at World Wide." As Claire began to clear the kitchen table, the land line phone rang. Claire walked to the kitchen wall and picked up the phone. "Hello? Mac, Good to hear from you. How did your day go?" Quietly she listened. "Yes, in fact, Dan is here now. She listened again. "He interviewed Alistair, and me."

Everyone in the room stopped talking, while Claire listened to her husband. "Sure." She turned to Dan. "He wants to talk to you." She handed him the phone.

"How goes it in jolly old England?" Then Dan listened. "So, you talked to him. Dinner with him, okay. No, I think you're right on with that idea. This case has grown much larger just since yesterday when you flew off to London." Dan listened again. "I'll check in with the Salt Lake office tomorrow. Watch your back. Did you pack a weapon? Good. Talk to you tomorrow."

Dan handed the phone back to Claire. "Hi." She nodded at the phone. "Okay, Love you too. Talk to you tomorrow." She turned and faced the people in her kitchen. "Alistair, it isn't safe for you to return to England just yet. It looks like you are going to be my houseguest for a while longer."

Chapter Fifteen

Alistair felt deflated, but could only shake his head. "I really need to get back to work."

"Mac said that he would send you a secure email through Hugh McIntire of Scotland Yard tomorrow. They will let you know how the investigation is proceeding." Claire said.

"Before we go, I'd like a copy of the infamous disc." Dan said." Angela, can you fetch the computer?"

"I'll get it." Alistair stomped upstairs to the room where he was staying. Returning, he set the disc down on the table. "Pretty soon the only people who won't have a copy of this disc are the bad guys."

Dan began to copy the disc. Soon he had downloaded the contents and returned the original to Alistair. Dan stood, shook Alistair's hand and waved at Claire. "We'd better go. We've two hours of storm to drive through. Thanks, Claire, for the pie and your hospitality."

Claire walked the two agents to the front door. "Oh look, it's snowing. You drive carefully."

"Snowing? I thought it was too warm here to snow?" Alistair hurried out onto the porch, and put his hand out to catch the flakes. The snow seemed to evaporate when it hit the roadway, but large flakes were falling into patterns of white on the lawn. He was dazzled by the storm. He wanted to go for a walk, and let the snow sink into his hair.

Claire came to stand beside him. "Come in Al, I don't want you to catch a cold." She held the door open for him to walk through. She closed and locked it. "I want you to recover from that wound without any setbacks."

One A.M. London, December 28th

Was it inspiration, blessings from above, or just plain luck that kept Mac awake after he returned from his visit with McIntire at Scotland Yard? He was dog tired, but this case kept swirling around in his brain, keeping him from any sleep.. He tried television, but British humor on the late-night talk shows, did little to entertain him. He had called Claire around midnight and had a chance to also talk to Dan.

An hour later he found himself brushing his teeth, and staring at his red rimmed eyes. The bed and sleep finally seemed to call to him. Because of the room's small size, the queen-sized bed had been placed kitty corner near the window and radiator.

Just to be on the safe side, he shoved his Glock slightly under the bed close to the window side, farther away from the door. The radiator had been installed down the outside wall closer to the bathroom door. He didn't quite close the drape across the window, which allowed a sliver of light to come into the room.

He had been in bed around fifteen minutes, when the sound of someone picking the lock of his door alerted him. He dived off the bed onto the floor near the wall, but jumped up and quickly made a body shaped mound with the pillows under the duvet.

Less than a minute later the lock clicked, and the door opened. A rather small hand reached around the door to release the night chain. A figure in dark clothing stepped into the room, and fired two shots at the pillows. The gun was equipped with a silencer.

The smaller man said. "Blimy, all you shot was feathers."

Mac dived across the bed and smacked the shooter with the butt of his Glock, sending the man's weapon flying against the wall. The noisy one swung his fist at Mac, but ended up on the floor with a large bare foot across his neck. Mac reached for his cell phone and dialed McIntire's cell number.

"McIntire, I've just had a couple of uninvited guests in my hotel room. Would you mind sending the paddy wagon for them?" Mac tied up the shooter with his handcuffs, and the talker with his belt.

Wearily, he pulled on his slacks, and sat in the only chair, with his weapon trained on the intruders.

Two officers stormed into the room about ten minutes later. Mac watched as they dragged out the shooter. He appeared to be Asian, and the other guy was a local thug.

McIntire came just then. "Take them to holding, boys." He said to his two officers. "I'm not about to interview them until morning." He turned to Mac. "Since you've come to town, neither of us has managed any sleep. I could take you home with me. I have an empty bedroom you could use."

Mac shook his head. "I was looking forward to spending eight or nine hours in that bed. I tried it out for a few hours earlier, and it's quite comfortable." He closed his eyes for a minute. "Do you have any of that crime scene tape? In the States it's yellow."

McIntire picked up his small bag and produced a roll of it. For a moment he just stared at it, but then a smile of recognition crossed his face. "You want me to tape up the door to this room?" He began to laugh. "Anything, so both of us can get some sleep. See you in the late morning. Better yet, come over to the 'yard' for some lunch."

They both walked to the door. Mac closed and locked it, and he could hear McIntire tear and mount the tape on the other side.

Eight Thirty, Mountain Standard Time,

After dinner Alistair turned to Claire. "Mind if I use the house phone. I want to call Jenna. Just to see how her day went." He shrugged, and dropped his eyes.

"Go ahead. I'm going to work on some inventory for the clinic." She went into the den and turned on her computer.

Alistair dialed Jenna's cell phone and she answered on the second ring. "Jenna, how are you?"

"Alistair, where are you? Did you fly back to England?" He could hear the concern in her voice.

"No, I'm here in St. George with Claire. Mac is still in London." He cleared his throat. "How did you presentation go?"

"It went really well. They really liked it, and this afternoon, we brain stormed to design a clever pamphlet to advertise it. We also asked the company to change their website slightly. "We're trying to come up with a 'catch phrase'."

"Catch phrase?" Alistair asked.

"Something to go on the pamphlet, that would catch people's attention; Especially those who would enjoy a rustic, 'outdoorzy' vacation. On another subject, how's your shoulder?"

"It's still sore, and my arm movement is restricted, but the pain is much less. I'm sure Claire's ministrations have- - - - - -, Jenna, I really miss you." He paused, took a deep breath. "I wish we could meet again before I return home."

"I'd like to see you, too." Her voice dropped, and she sniffed. "Maybe if you have to stay a while longer- - - -?" Her voice broke and he could hear her crying.

"Please don't cry, Jenna. I'm not worth your tears." Alistair sighed.

"Sorry," She sniffed. He heard her set the phone down. A moment later, she then picked it up. "I've just had a crazy day. The thugs tried to kidnap me this morning."

"What! Where! What happened?" He asked, for a moment he was frantic with worry.

"It happened on the elevator, early this morning. I parked on the fifth level at the Town Mall and was carrying all my stuff for the presentation. I got into the elevator, and these two goons pushed their way in, and one grabbed me. The FBI rescued me. It was really scary, but rather exciting too. Anyway, the thugs were arrested for kidnapping. One of them dug his nails into my arm. The CSU came and photographed it."

"Oh, dear girl, look at all the trouble I've caused you. I can't begin-- - - - - -"

"You've had troubles too. You must keep a positive attitude. That will help you'll heal faster."

"Claire is going to make sure I recuperate properly. I wanted to go stand in the snow storm and she dragged me back inside the house." He chuckled.

"It snowed in Rawley? The white stuff is falling here, but that's to be expected this time of year. When do you think you'll fly home?"

"Not until Mac says it's safe." He answered.

"Well, now I know where you are, I'll keep in touch. Miss you Al."

"Miss you too, Jenna. Get some rest, good night."

Alistair had been in bed for what seem half the night, but sleep would not come. With drapes open he could see the cloudy sky. It wasn't pain or even discomfort that kept him awake, it was thinking about Jenna. Could he be moving toward being in love with her? Can one fall in love with a girl in three days? He closed his eyes, but what he saw were those flashing blue eyes, and that soft blonde hair falling to her shoulders. And of course that trim, curvaceous body.

More than her physical attributes settled in his mind. She was strong, stable and had a sense of adventure, and she could cook. What more could a man ask for? He could not walk away from this, yet fragile relationship. He wanted it to strengthen, and have it continued.

December 28th Six a.m. London

Rutledge's personal phone jangled him from a sound sleep. He reached over on his bedside table for the offending noise. He answered with a curt. "What the devil is it?"

"Mr. Rutledge." The man with an overly correct British accent said. "It seems that your people have failed in their assignment to negate the American irritation, and did not get the disc. We must now move to our alternate plan."

"You're ready to take over the Lorry? Do you have enough people for the job?"

Rutledge's wife stirred, and he turned away from her, and sat up on the edge of the bed.

"Yes, and we need the exact coordinates by late this afternoon."

"Yes, all right. I'll call you this afternoon. Do you have someone to fly the plane?"

"Your only concern should be the exact route of lorry will take. We'll do the rest." The phone call ended with a dial tone in Rutledge's ear.

A hand touched Rutledge's back, and he twisted around as if he had been burned. "Who's calling so early?" His wife asked in a soft, sleepy voice.

"Just a problem at the plant, and now I must take care of it." He stood and slipped his feet into leather slippers, and grabbed up a soft velour robe. "Go back to sleep."

An hour later Howard Rutledge sat at his desk and booted up his computer. He carefully checked the route of the particular lorry carrying a load of fine wines, expensive liquor, tea, coffee and gourmet chocolate.

CHAPTER SIXTEEN

The truck's original route was to the docks of Liverpool. The cargo was scheduled to be loaded onto the ship bound for Miami, Florida. There, awaited a larger ship. It was the largest cruise ship ever built, and was ready to be christened, and begin its maiden voyage. Its agenda was for the South Atlantic and on to tropical destinations.

Rutledge swiveled his large leather chair, and stared out into the still nearly dark, leaden sky. No one was there to bring him his morning coffee and English muffin. Finally, he rose and went to the small bar tucked into an area on the right side of his office. There he found an electric water heater, a mug and instant coffee. He grimaced at the first sip of the now liquefied grains, but all he could find was synthetic cream, no sugar. This was the extent of his morning comforts.

As he sat down, he rang up his man at the warehouse. "Terry, its Rutledge. The Lorry in question needs to go out this afternoon. Who's to drive the truck?"

"Jumper, he'll be in this morning. We'll take care of it. Just remember we're taking twenty percent of the wine as our pay. We'll drive it to the spot we picked, and then turn to the place where will they can take over and drive on to the airstrip."

"You're taking twenty percent?" Rutledge scowled.

"It won't be on the truck, and so they'll never miss it. What time do we meet them?"

"Four- thirty P. M. This afternoon. Be there."

"What are those NK's planning to do with all that fine food? We could find a buyer for the lot of it, quick and easy."

"Just close the deal." Rutledge slammed down the phone.

Mid-day December 28th, London

Mac sauntered into Scotland Yard close to lunchtime. A Ms. Saunders directed him into Inspector McIntire's office.

"Please have a seat. May I get you anything?' She asked with a smile.

As he rubbed his eyes, still groggy from nearly nine hours of sleep, he looked up. "I wouldn't mind some coffee." While he waited, he marveled at the modern structure that now was Scotland Yard. From large windows one could gaze out at the River Thames many stories below. The London sky was cloudy, but a slim area showed a slice of blue sky.

Ms. Saunders returned with a small tray and set it on McIntire's desk. It contained coffee, a plate with a toasted English muffin along with a small side portion of butter, and jam.

Mac grinned at the trim, dark-haired girl in gray sweater and slacks. "This is first rate. Thank you." She backed out, of the office, smiled and left him alone to sip and munch.

As the food went down, his eyes, mind, and mood brightened. A few minutes later, McIntire walked in and dropped a thick file as well as a large gun in a plastic bag. He also carried another smaller bag and set it on his desk.

"Is that the weapon you grabbed last night along with the two perps?" Mac asked.

"Yes, I've one of them in the room right now for questioning. You want to observe?"

"Absolutely." Mac grinned and followed the inspector. He was waved into a chair next to a large two-way mirror.

"Have a seat. You may enjoy this, and see how it compares to your standard interrogation techniques used in America."

McIntire walked into the small concrete room and to the rectangular table. A small man sat hand cuffed on the opposite side. The inspector dropped the large file and the hand gun on the table with a thunk. "Well now, Mr. John Slade, is it?"

A small man, probably in his forties, shifted his posture. "I don't know no Slade."

"Interesting,- - - - - - -, your fingerprints on the lock picking kit tell us a different story." McIntire waved the bagged kit at the prisoner.

Slade stared at the small kit. "I was carrying it, that's all." He slumped down unto the hard metal chair.

"Your prints are all over the outside _and_ the inside of the kit. Also, we found them on the doorknob, and on the outside of the hotel room door. It's where we found a boot print. Your boot print."

Slade glanced down at his stocking covered, shoeless feet. "So's I got inside the room, that's all." He grimaced. "Me back hurts where that American bloke stood on it while trussin me up."

"We'll give you an aspirin later. What were you doing in Mr. MacCandlass' room?"

"Openin' the door for another bloke. He needed to get in." Slade said.

"And why was that?' McIntire glared at the little man.

"I dunno, just did. That's why we went there, to get in."

"Yes, you did. Your plan was to kill Mr. MacCandlass." The inspector stood up and grabbed Slade's shirt, and dragged him inches from his face.

"I didn't go there to kill nobody. Linn had the gun." The words came out in a rush.

"So, which one of you shot into the bed clothes, thinking it was a sleeping man?"

"Not me, I jus' open the door."

"You'd better start explaining everything, or you'll not only be charged with a breaking and entering, but also attempted murder." McIntire growled at his prisoner. He dropped back in the chair.. "With your multiple felony convictions, one more and you'll die behind gray cement walls. Who hired you? Why were you working with Linn Huong?"

"I'm hungry, un my back's killing me." Slade whined.

"If we can have a satisfactory discussion here, we'll let you have some lunch, and an aspirin or two." McIntire softened his voice.

Slade sighed. "Linn called me said the American had something they wanted."

"They? Did he say who they were?" Who was paying you?"

"Linn handed me forty quid. 'Said the job was quick and easy. Just break into the Yank's hotel room." He looked down at his shoeless feet, and grimaced. "Me feet's cold. Now I think I need a lawyer."

"We'll see about that." McIntire sighed, and motioned to the young officer standing by the door. He picked Slade out of the chair, and marched him away. McIntire picked up the file, the two plastic bags, and walked out of the interview room.

"That didn't take too long, and was relatively easy. I'll go after Linn later today." He nodded to Mac, and they walked back into McIntire's office. "Ms. Saunders." He called.

"Yes sir." She hurried into his office.

"Take these items to property, and file this." He pointed to Slade's fat file. "Time for a hearty lunch. Let's go." He put his hand on Mac's shoulder.

Ten A.M. December 28th, Salt Lake City

After a Google search listing several Tina Woo's, Higby decided to call the address the girl had listed on her admission papers. He asked his director for permission to call Hong Kong.

"Go ahead Bill. Make the call to the girl's parents." Director Carlson said.

"This is FBI agent, William Higby., calling from the United States. I was wondering if I could take a few moments of you time."

A woman answered the phone in a clipped British accent. "Yes, I'm Mrs. Woo. What information can do you need?"

"I'm calling in regards to your daughter Tina Woo."

"My daughter? What are you talking about?" The woman's voice rose in concern.

"A Tina Woo. I met the girl yesterday. She is a student at the University in Provo, Utah, USA. She lists her home address as the one I am calling. I'd like to know how long she has been in The United States, and the state of Utah. Higby asked.

"This is impossible!" The woman's voice was close to hysterical.

Higby heard her voice crack, and another voice in the background. Then he heard both voices talking in rapid Chinese.

A masculine voice came on the line. "Mr. Higby, is it? I'm Chan Woo. There has been some mistake. Our daughter Tina was killed in an automobile accident three years ago."

Higby sucked in a large breath as he took quick notes."I'm so sorry for your loss, Mr. Woo. Now we believe this girl we are investigating here, is using your daughter's identity. My partner and I met her yesterday.

Is there some item that your daughter owned that would still have her fingerprints on it? One of your police officers could collect it from you, and check the fingerprints on the item. They can send the results to us, and the information can be entered into an international database."

"Because of her accident, there was an autopsy. The police should have the report with her fingerprints on it. I'm sure I could request that information. They should also have a copy of her driver's license." Chan Woo said.

"Again, I am sorry to have bothered you. Thank you so much for the information."

Higby set the phone back into its cradle. "Well, I'll be damned." He sat back and rubbed his buzz cut hair. Soon he jumped up and hurried into Carlson's office. "I need to contact the Hong Kong police, and I need a warrant to search our local Tina Woo's dorm room."

Four-thirty p.m., Near Liverpool, England
December 28th

The lorry proceeded down a narrow bumpy road. It's manifest read: *deliver to dock # eighteen,* Liverpool docks'. Yet the Lorry turned south rather than continue on to the docks. Jumper was driving, chewing on a cigar stub, and grinning like the proverbial cat, which had just lapped up the cream. "We're goin' ta make a nice haul on those cases of wine we left in the warehouse. Mark my words."

"How much, Jumper? I need a fix when we get back." Terry asked.

"More un enough for a dozen fixes. We'll deliver this load and be back, 'fore supper." Jumper turned again down a gravel road rutted from the recent rain, barely visible winding through a frozen meadow and the approaching fog. Suddenly, as he drove, he realized he was close, but yet could barely see the outline of a plane sitting on a short runway. Only soft red landing lights were visible in the thickening fog. He identified it as an older B737, waiting on the blacktop. This was a good hiding place, out in the middle of this frozen field.

Chapter Seventeen

A man with a powerful flashlight waved them around to the left side of the plane. "Back up." He yelled, and Jumper did as he was directed. Once he stopped the lorry, it listed half on and half off the tarmac. Jumper brought it in tight, and shut down the engine. He and Terry jumped out of the truck. Jumper went to the rear, and raised the lift gate. The two of them began to unload the contents of the truck, in small crates. Piling them on hand trucks .and pushing them to two ramps set up close to the open doorways of the plane. The heavier, larger boxes, they carefully carried, and left them at the base of the ramps. Two men inside carried them into the plane.

Jumper could see that the plane had been gutted to hold as much cargo as possible, with only four first class seats remaining, close to the front.

When the lorry was nearly empty, Jumper noticed that flashlight man had a clipboard with a checklist on it. As Terry carried the last crate to the rear door of the plane, flashlight man asked. Where are the missing twenty cases?"

"That's our cut for bringing this load to you." Terry grinned, but before he could even react, the man pulled out a small caliber weapon from his pocket and pumped two bullets into Terry's chest.

Jumper didn't wait around, but began running across the meadow toward a stand of trees about thirty meters away. Flashlight man fired again, and Jumper felt a burning pain in his right side and again in his shoulder. He staggered a few feet, but finally, he dropped and lay still. All the while his blood dripped into the frozen field.

*****

The three men began an argument in a language Jumper couldn't understand, but knew it was either Chinese or Korean.

Flashlight man got into the lorry and drove it into the meadow on an angle, leaving the door open. The other two pulled up the rear ramp and shut the rear doors of the plane. Flashlight man ran to the plane climbed aboard, pulled up the ramp and closed the front door. The plane's engines came to life, and soon Jumper could hear the plane begin its takeoff.

Jumper tried to get up, and once he made it to his knees, but then dropped on his face on the hard, cold meadow. He was so very cold, and could not find the strength to stand, so he knelt there. He heard the plane take off, but couldn't get back up so he lay back down. The frozen ground underneath him didn't feel quite so cold anymore, and his eyes were heavy. He felt so tired. Maybe, for a moment or two, he would take a little nap.

Mid-afternoon, Mountain Time, Salt Lake December 28th.

A girl in a white coat came to Higby's desk and handed him the results of Tina Woo's fingerprint analysis. He swiveled his chair toward Balfour's desk. "Here is the fingerprint comparison on Tina Woo, from CU. The original Tina did not rise from the grave. We're dealing here with two Tina Woo's, one dead and the other an impostor. We need to get back to Provo and pick up the phony Tina, pronto." He walked into his director's office and showed him the fingerprint results.

Director Carlson came out of his office. "I think we need to have a chat with this girl in Provo. I wonder how carefully the University down there checks out their foreign students."

*****

When the two FBI agents reached Tina Woo's dorm room, it took them several minutes to find the floor monitor, who carried a pass key. "Thank you for letting us into the room." Higby said.

The girl wanted to hang around to see what they would find in their search. "Thank you, Ms. Grayson, we'll let you know when we're finished."

"Okay, you're sure you don't need me? I'd be glad to stay." She leaned in the doorway with her arms folded, but she sighed, and stepped back allowing to Balfour close the door.

They made a quick search of the room. They could see Tina had left in a hurry. First thing missing was her laptop. Higby traced the place on her desk where it had been. Also, they could not find a suitcase, duffle bag, winter coat, or even the sweater she had worn the day before.

Balfour folded his large frame into the student desk chair. "She left in a hurry. I wonder if she's headed for Salt Lake International. I'm calling Johnson. He could get out there and look for her."

"He needs to know who to look for. Look in the desk, maybe you'll find a picture." Balfour rolled back the chair and began a search of the desk. Higby began a check of the book shelves.

"Ah ha." He held up a small photo album. In it he found a picture of the whole staff of _Ultimate Batteries._ "Get him on the phone and we'll send this to him."

In the desk drawer he found a note pad. From the writing indentations he could see the top page had been torn off. He took a pencil from the desk drawer, began to shade the paper with the writing tool.

Higby glanced at the pad. "What is that detective assignment 101?"

"Don't laugh." Balfour held up the pad. And then Higby could read: Delta fl. 1226. 3:40.

"Call Johnson, give him the information. Maybe he can catch her."

Balfour called Agent Johnson, already on his way to the airport. "Hi, I sending you Tina Woo's picture."

"Okay, got it. Oh, by the way, if I catch her? What do I charge her with?"

"Identity theft and it's a good chance she's in this country illegally." Higby said.

"Okay, the identity theft is Hong Kong's problem, and being an illegal is ICE's problem. I don't believe either behavior is a federal offense." Johnson said in his bland, but deep voice. "You guys will need to find something else, and fast."

Balfour shook his head. "He's right. However, Incriminating evidence may be on her computer."

"I can't grab her computer unless I *know* something illegal is on it." Johnson said.

"If you can find her, hold her. We're going back to Batteries Ultimate Corp. "

*****

It took nearly half an hour for the two agents to drive back to the warehouse home of _Ultimate Batteries, Corp._ Tina was not at work, but neither Balfour nor Higby neither expected to find her there. They did find Paul Reacher.

"Well hi, you guys, you're back again?' Reacher said, his little smile did not reach his eyes, and he seemed wary.

"Yes, we'd like to take a look at Tina's work station." Balfour said.

"Of course, it's over here. She called me at home, early this morning, and said she had a family emergency. I didn't think she had any family in the U.S."

"What we've uncovered, she doesn't. Would you boot up her computer?" Higby asked.

"Sure," The little smile turned into a frown. "She has a password on this. I'm not sure- - - - -. Markus, do you know Tina's password?"

"What's John's middle name?" Markus wiggled his eyebrows.

"John's middle name is- - - - -, William." The password worked and they got into her files. "What are you searching for?" Paul asked.

"Anything that shouldn't be here. Ah, here's an email to Chin Whah." The email read:

Specs must be tested, incomplete. I doubt girl has them. Get out while you can. Tina

"We'll be taking the computer to our lab. We'll give you a receipt for it." Balfour produced a notebook, and wrote out a receipt and asked Paul to sign it.

"Is Tina coming back?" Paul asked, with concern in his voice.

Higby just shook his head. "We'll be arresting her quite soon."

Markus came over and put his hand on Paul's shoulder. "Sorry buddy, John shouldn't have become so tight with her."

The two agents nodded and hauled out the tower of Tina's computer.

As Claire slipped into a jacket to go out for some lunch, her office phone rang. She scowled at the noisy instrument. She was starving and was looking forward to a Subway sandwich. "Southern Dixie Animal Clinic, Claire speaking."

"Claire this is Dan. The two perps who tried to kidnap Jenna are going to be arraigned tomorrow afternoon. But before that can happen, we have to have Jenna, and even Alistair to pick them out of a group of four or five guys similar to them, in other words, a line up. I need to take Alistair with me tomorrow morning to Salt Lake."

"That would be good for him, poor guy. He's so bored. If he has to sit inside my house one more day, he might become desperate enough to read a romance novel. He's already read a mystery novel by John Grisham. What time, tomorrow?"

"Early, about six A.M. That will get us to the federal building by ten- thirty A.M. Angela and I will escort him, and be with him the whole time."

"Alistair told me about Jenna's experience. I hope you can nail these guys. I'll have him up and ready to go."

"We believe at least one of these guys were one of two perps who shot Alistair, and chased Jenna and him all over Salt Lake County. If we can identify at least one of them, it will strengthen our case against them. The North Korean Consulate is screaming for their release. They wanted them arraigned this morning. Another lead is the Asian girl who worked for *Ultimate Batteries, Corp.* We know she's in the country illegally."

"Wow, Mac will want to know all this. That's why he went to London, to find out which side of the Atlantic is *dirty*. It now could be both." Claire said. 'However, I think I'll let you update him."

"Most likely, but I think it started in the U.K." Dan said. "Thanks for your help, Claire. "We'll see you tomorrow."

Claire hurried back from the Subway with her sandwich. It had begun to rain, not unusual for St. George in winter, but her short raincoat wouldn't button over her growing midsection, and so she had worn a fleece jacket that morning, and it didn't keep her dry. She tried a loping run, to stay dry and get into back to the clinic. She settled at her desk in the tiny cubicle she called her office, when the phone rang again. Once of her assistants picked it up.

"Claire the phone's for you. I think it's Mac." The girl giggled.

Claire picked up. "Hi guy, how are you?" Claire said. "What time is it there?"

"About eight- thirty P.M. I just came back from having some fish and chips. They really know how to fix that meal here. It ranks up there as very good. How are you getting along with our houseguest?"

"Alistair's getting stronger every day, and I'm fine. Dan is picking him up early tomorrow morning and driving him to Salt Lake. Alistair is going to be looking at a line-up, to try and identify the shooters in said lineup. They are the ones who tried to snatch Jenna. Dan's coming *really* early." Claire laughed.

"I hope they can make those charges stick this time. I need to stay here long enough to see if Scotland Yard can build a case against Rutledge. I'm almost acclimated to the fog, and rain, but not quite. Take it easy, I love you and that fetus you're sheltering. So I'll say goodbye for now."

"Love you too, Bye." Claire set down the phone with a sigh.

*****

Mac had just settled in to watch the American movie channel. They were playing a John Travolta film he hadn't seen. Ten minutes into the film, his phone rang.

"McIntire, here. We've been called out to a crime scene. A lorry has been, as you American's say, hi-jacked. Its destination was the Liverpool docks. You want to take a look?"

"Why, what's the connection?" Mac asked.

"The lorry was carrying gourmet food and drink, but it originated from a warehouse owned by our Mr. Rutledge. Plus, the two blokes driving the truck are lying in a meadow, quite dead."

"When will you be here?" Mac was definitely intrigued.

"Twenty minutes. Wear your boots and a muffler."

Chapter Eighteen

When in England in the winter time, a Las Vegas/St. George wardrobe was found to be, in a word, inadequate. Mac decided to make it his best effort to stay warm. He went downstairs to the little shop in the hotel called _Scottish Woolens, Limited._ He found the shop shuttered for the night, but with a request at the front desk, a young woman soon came to open it.

Fifteen minutes later he had purchased a woolen pullover sweater, a pair of tan cords, and a delicate purple sweater for Claire. He rushed up to his room, and along with the turtle neck, he put on the sweater and slacks. After boots, heavy socks, and his lined rain coat he was ready. At the last minute he searched his suitcase for the scarf Claire had given him for Christmas.

As he stomped out onto the curb, McIntire plus two other officers were waiting in a formidable Range Rover. It was foggy for starters, and once they left to M-5 carriage way, the fog was like a big wet blanket. McIntire managed to negotiate narrow roads at speeds that Mac knew were over the limit. And to top it all off he kept up a rambling conversation the whole time.

"The locals left the two dead blokes where they dropped. So, we have a chance to view the crime scene, not too stomped upon." The inspector said.

Soon they reached a narrow dirt road and, McIntire parked at the west end of the meadow. With a cursory examination, Mac noticed that one of the victims had been shot twice in the chest, and lay close to what looked like an airplane landing strip. Mac grabbed the flashlight from one of the officers, and traced landing gear tracks down this runway. This field was several miles from the commercial airport in Liverpool.

McIntire came over to Mac. "The first corpse you've checked out is, I believe, named Terry Comer. Over here, take a look at the other one." He led Mac across the field near a corpse of trees. "This one took the bullets, I think, near an artery and bled out. He works for Rutledge, but off hand I don't remember his name, and won't know until we get them back to autopsy. As McIntire was speaking, a wagon from the local medical examiners' pulled into the area near the lorry and one man jumped out.

"Inspector, you ready for us to take the stiffs?"

*****

McIntire nodded, and waved the two men over and stepped out of the way. "Now, time to search the lorry, at least as much as this fog and darkness will allow."

Mac followed the inspector, and climbed into the back of the truck. "Here's a torn label from a box of Black Label Scotch. Definitely high-end cargo." Mac said.

McIntire grabbed the manifest clipped to spot in the cab, and handed it to Mac. "We'll lock up this truck, and return with the Crime Scene Team tomorrow. We can't do much more in the dark and this 'pea soup'."

Mac was stiff with cold, and his legs seemed to only move at a slow pace. He followed the two officers and the Inspector back to the Range Rover. Once they all climbed in and McIntire started up the heater, Mac finally had feeling in his feet and his tense back and shoulders could relax.

"Oh, slipped my mind. The Mrs. has been concerned for your comfort." McIntire handed his guest a sack. In the bag Mac pulled out a soft woolen, tweed cap with a brim. Mac tried it on, and smiled. It was just what he needed.

Eight a.m., December 29th, London

Three rapid knocks brought Mac out of the bathroom. Carefully he opened the door. "Ah inspector, come in."

McIntire stomped in and set a large, paper cup of coffee on the small table close to the door. "Let us move quickly back to the crime scene. With the heavy traffic, it will take us longer this morning, than it took us last evening to reach the scene of the crime. Put on your warm socks, because it is a raw morning. It's possible we'll have snow before the day is through."

"I planned on it being cold out there." Mac sat on the chair and laced up his boots. After that he donned the trench coat and his new woolen cap. He dug into coat pocket and produced a pair of leather gloves.

"If you stay here long enough young man, you'll begin to dress English." McIntire laughed.

The inspector had been correct. The morning traffic was typical of any large city in the U.S. Finally, they reached the field and the crime scene. The frozen meadow had a tinge of silver frost covering it, and it crunched underfoot.

Mac focused on the landing site. He carefully examined the landing gear tracks, now slick with frost, and paced the length of the runway. As the inspector jumped down from the lorry, Mac glanced up. "The plane that took off from this cleverly hidden, but rather short runway couldn't be any larger than a B737. The tarmac is too short. Also, it would take a certifiably talented pilot, who managed to get the plane in the air."

McIntire joined Mac. "This, my young American friend, is a break through. This must be the place where the heroin suppliers flew in with their cargo. Before today, we could never solve the problem of how the drugs were brought into England."

"The plane could be registered to North Korea, but not necessarily. It could be some other country or individual willing to register it. Willing to ignore the fact that this plane could possibly be used to fly in contraband. Or ignore the official use of the plane." Mac said.

Both of them looked up as another car rumbled down the narrow road. "Ah, our crew to move the lorry has arrived. I believe we're finished here. Time to find a good cafe and enjoy a proper English breakfast." McIntire led the way back to the Range Rover.

McIntire picked a noisy, busy cafe near an exit from the M-5 Carriageway leading to back to London. They soon were sitting at a corner table with most of surface covered with steaming dishes of food and coffee. Some of them Mac even recognized.

As Mac took a bite of warm, buttered, wheat toast, he smiled and chewed. After a sip of coffee, he asked. "When do we spring all of our suppositions on Rutledge?"

"We'll make a 'we have information' visit to our Mr. Rutledge this afternoon."

Two-thirty p. m, December 29th, London

"Mr. Rutledge, you have a call on line two." His secretary, Ms. Thorne buzzed him.

"Mr. Rutledge, this is Tom Saunders, from the warehouse."

"Yes, what is it?' Rutledge was upset and his voice showed it.

"The lorry bound for Liverpool never arrived. We've had calls from the dock, and the ship the cargo was bound for sailed at noon. Terry and Jumper took it out and we've not seen either one of them since yesterday afternoon."

Rutledge knew what had happened to the lorry, but where were Jumper and Terry?

"Sir, do you want me to call the authorities?" Saunders asked.

"Not yet. I'll make some calls. They could be anywhere between here and Liverpool. Thank you for the call, Saunders. Good day." Rutledge moved away from his desk and began to pace. Where could those two worthless blokes be? Probably bartering a case of wine for drugs, and women. That's where they were, in some brothel in Liverpool. He reasoned.

Rutledge nervously began to pace the length of his luxury office.

He was losing control of his life. A few months ago, everything was fine. The work at the plant was going along as scheduled. Even Powell's trip to the United States was somewhat according to plan, but the North Korean's began demanding more and more money for their shipments. He was forced to take some of their kind into his organization. They insisted he order those batteries from the U.S. more than he would need for a few prototypes.

Trying to kill Powell for the plans on the disc was foolhardy. Soon Fat, the local leader he was forced to deal with, demanded the information from Ultimate Batteries, organization, and Rutledge did not yet have it. Of course, he did not tell them that little bit of information. Now because of the attack on Alistair Powell, he had an FBI agent and Inspector McIntire on his heels.

His phone buzzed again. "Mr. Rutledge, Masseurs McIntire and MacCandlass are here to see you." A spear of fear jagged through him, and he was forced to grab the corner of his desk for support.

"Give me a moment." He hurried to his small lavatory behind the bar in his office and splashed water on his face, and patted down his thinning hair. He straightened his tie, and buttoned his suit coat. He glanced around his office, and knew his lavish lifestyle was coming to an end.

He sat behind his desk and busied himself with some papers. MacCandlass, and McIntire strolled in as if they had all the time in the world to cross to his desk. "Gentlemen, come in, come in." He managed to stand, though his knees trembled, and the smile he pasted on his face was thin. At least he managed to shake their hands. "Please have a seat. What can I do for you two this afternoon?" He slumped back in his fine leather, upholstered chair.

"The Liverpool police contacted me last night with the news that one of the Lorry's from your warehouse was found robbed and abandoned."

"You found it? I had news that it was missing not long before you came in." He tried for a look of surprise.

"Yes." The inspector went on. "It had been emptied of its cargo and your two drivers, I must inform you, were found dead at the scene." The inspector had a grim expression.

"Oh, terrible, terrible. I was informed they were missing, but- - - - -? Was it accidental?"

"No, they were murdered." McIntire said in a flat voice.

*****

Mac sat back and watched Rutledge react to the information about the Lorry. He could sense the Inspector stringing Rutledge along.

"So now sir, why were your drivers found in a rural area, and in the middle of that field where a clandestine air strip had been built? They were miles from the Port of Liverpool, their official destination. The inspector's voice was without emotion, but strong.

"In a field? I don't- - - - - -? They must have been misguided, or forced to drive there." Rutledge's face was now slick with sweat, and he mopped his brow with a large white handkerchief.

"Right now, as we speak, several of my officers have served a warrant at your warehouse. We'll be checking to see if any of the cargo on the manifest is still in the building, along with anything else of interest they may find." McIntire drove home his points.

"Warehouse, you have no right. You can't do this. What reason- - - - - -?"

The inspector cut him off. "We also have in custody two men who tried to kill Mr. MacCandlass. They broke into his room, and shot at what they thought was his sleeping form. We can link these men to your ring of thieves, dealers of illegal substances."

"Gang of thieves? I had no idea.- - - - -."

At that moment, the inspector's cell phone rang. "Yes?' He listened. "Good, I'll see you at the 'yard'." He snapped his phone shut. "Stand up Rutledge; you're under arrest for possession of stolen property and illegal substances."

As the three men strolled out of Rutledge's office with him in handcuffs, Ms. Thorn stood and watched with mouth agape. "What should I do, sir?" She asked in a quavering voice.

"Call my attorney. Tell I've been taken to Scotland Yard!"

On their way to the 'yard', Mac casually asked McIntire a question. "Do you have a gymnasium, or work-out area I could use?"

"Yes, there is such in an adjacent building, on level three. There is exercise equipment, a running track and a swimming pool. If you like I can grant you pass to gain entrance."

"I've been here three days, and I really need a work-out." Mac said.

"Sounds like a fine idea, I may join you. Have you ever played hand ball?"

Chapter Nineteen

Eight A.M. Mountain Standard Time, December 29th

When Dan left the freeway at Fillmore, Utah, he drove into the parking lot near a *Carl's Junior Restaurant.*

Alistair riding the back seat was jolted awake. He had been in a drowsy sleep shortly after leaving Rawley. After Dan picked him up, they had traveled north at freeway speeds without stopping.

"We're about half way to Salt Lake. So, this is a bathroom stop, as well as a place to pick up a little breakfast." Dan climbed out of the big Chevrolet Suburban and walked into the restaurant, with Angela following on his heels.

Alistair climbed out and stretched. Immediately he felt the bitter cold, yet with a hint of a sunrise to the east. He made for the warmth of the building. A few minutes later the three of them were back in the vehicle. This time Angela took the wheel. All of them had breakfast sandwiches of one type or another, and each a beverage of choice. Alistair found a more comfortable seat behind Angela, because she was smaller than Dan and had moved the seat up closer to drive.

He stared out the window, and found this part of Utah had the unrelenting scenery of snow-covered fields with mountains to the east. They drove for several miles with little change in scenery. He tried to go back to sleep, but could not, because he began to think of Jenna. He would be able to see her in just a few hours.

Angela found a soft rock station on the radio, and Dan dozed. An hour or so later they drove past the town of Nephi. When driving down to St. George with Claire, they had stopped there. That place must be named for some Biblical character. He would have to look it up.

Because Angela kept the car moving at a steady eighty miles per hour, they seemed to fly by several small towns. After a while the towns they passed became larger and he could see more suburban growth and sprawl along the sides of the freeway. Big box stores, markets and fast-food outlets of many varieties clustered close to the roadways. Housing seemed to be farther away, and groups of them were built on the hills to the east. To the west was he could see a large lake.

Angela had to drop her speed, because the traffic became heavier. Yet, she managed to keep up with the flow of traffic, and once she reached the pass lane, she could pick up her speed. Finally at the Sixth South off ramp they left the freeway and drove east, into down town Salt Lake City. She slowed, and drove across a street into an underground parking area. He managed to see a large building of gray stone and brick, as they drove underneath it. Finally, they parked.

When Alistair exited the car, at first, he was stiff and sore, but moving his body in a regular walking gate felt good. They went to an elevator which took them up three floors. They walked down a long hall with closed doors on either side. They were ushered into an anteroom with a large two-way mirror. The other side was dark.

There were folding chairs on each side of the room, which left the middle empty. A minute or so later, the door opened again, and in came a large African-American man in the usual dark suit, uniform of the FBI. He ushered in Jenna.

Alistair jumped to his feet. "Jenna" He took her hand and pulled her over to an empty chair next to his. "It's so good to see you." He moved close to her and just had to hug her.

The hug did not go unnoticed by Angela. "In the three days they spent together, it seems they managed to know each other quite well." She tilted her head toward the couple, but smiled at Dan.

"Oh, I must introduce you to Dan and Angela." Alistair pointed out his two protectors. "This is Dan Forester. He was Mac's partner last year, and his new partner, Angela Patton."

"My temporary protector is Rafe Johnson." Jenna waved her hand at the tall FBI agent.

Rafe stood. "What we're going to do people, is to for you, Jenna, and you Alistair, to study each man in the room on the other side of this mirror. When the light comes on in the adjoining room there should be four or five men standing there. They will not be able to see or hear you. Each one of them will have a number. If you want any of them to come closer to the mirror, you just call out his number. Would you please start Jenna?"

She stood close to the window, and Rafe said something into an inter-com built into the wall into the wall next to the mirror. The lights came on, and five Asian men walked in; each holding a number. They were all casually dressed, and faced the mirror.

Jenna studied them for a long moment. "Could I have number four come forward?" Johnson flipped the inter-com and requested the man walk closer. "Is it possible that I could I see his hands, like this?" She put up her hand's palms back, fingers extended. Johnson gave the order.

Number four did as he was asked. His facial expression turned menacing. He had very long polished fingernails. Jenna turned to Johnson. "He was the man who grabbed me in the elevator.at the parking garage."

Johnson clicked on the inter-com. "Guard, take out number four." The lights went out, but quickly came back on with a new man standing with the number four.

Alistair joined Jenna close to the mirror. "Okay Jenna, Alistair, do any of the others look familiar?" Rafe asked.

"May I have a small mirror?" Jenna said. Angela searched her handbag and handed Jenna compact with a mirror in it. "Please have number three come forward." Jenna turned her back to the window and studied the man through the mirror. "He looks very much like the man who leaned out of the passenger window, and shot at my car in Cottonwood. Yes, he was young, like that man."

"May I see that?" Alistair took the mirror from Jenna. He closed his eyes, trying to bring forth the image of the men chasing and shooting at him, as well as those in the black car. He then opened them. "Yes, he definitely was in the Black Mercedes behind Jenna and me in the parking garage. I'm not sure if he shot me, but he could have. There were two of them."

"Guard, number three." Said Johnson into the intercom. The remaining men shuffled out, and the room beyond the mirror became dark. "Thank you both. Now come with me and you can sign some forms." He opened the door, and the group followed him down the hall.

*****

Once they were finished, Dan spoke to them all. "How about some lunch?"

Alistair turned to Jenna. "Do you need to return to work?"

"Not right away. I'd love to go to lunch with you." She looked at Alistair, but then she glanced up, and cleared her throat. "All of you, of course." She blushed.

Dan drove them to a fast-food place a few blocks away, called *Crown Burgers*. It was a fairly large place, and quite busy. The FBI agents found places along the wall with a table between the bench and some chairs. Dan and Rafe took all their orders for sandwiches, picked up and then set the trays of food on the tables. Jenna opted for a salad rather than French fries with her sandwich, but Alistair wanted the fried potato strips, as he called them.

"Ymm, this is good!" Jenna said, and took another big bite, wiping her mouth with a napkin. "Good choice Dan."

Alistair studied his sandwich for a moment, but then took a bite. "I agree, quite tasty." He picked up a fry and chomped it down.

"Try it with fry sauce. Did you know this sauce was invented right here in Utah." Jenna said.

"Hmmm." Alistair dipped a potato slice into the sauce. "Interesting, quite good."

Dan dipped a fry in the sauce. "You're teasing, aren't you, Jenna?" She shook her head.

"That's Amazing." He laughed.

"I don't care where it was invented; because it tastes like it came from Alabama." Rafe said.

Jenna laughed, and continued eating.

Alistair touched her shoulder. "It's so good to see you relaxed. It's just good to see you,"

She leaned against him and his head was close to hers, and he couldn't resist kissing her. She picked up a napkin and wiped both their mouths.

He sat back. "I suppose it would be better if we don't kiss in the restaurant."

"Do you think we'll ever see the end of this 'caper' as Mac calls it?" Jenna had a serious look on her face.

Dan shifted in his chair. "I think we're close to building a fairly tight case, especially against the two Asian men. We have arrested the girl working at *Ultimate Batteries, Corp.* We're still 'light' on a motive. So far I don't understand why everyone wanted the disc. At least from what our techs say, is incomplete. Perhaps you're the one who can unlock the mystery, Alistair."

He glanced over at Dan with quizzical expression on his face. "How?"

"By building and combining a computer from your company with a suitable battery from the organization here in Utah. Then we could take a look at its capabilities, and possibilities."

Alistair had a thoughtful expression, but suddenly his face brightened. "Of course, we would need to explore what that combination could do, and how the NK's, as you call them, would plan to use such a prototype."

Jenna finished her food, glanced around the table and began

clearing it of empty hamburger boxes and paper napkins.

"Jenna, sit down, relax. You don't need to clean up after us.'" Alistair pulled her down back onto the bench. "Come, sit down, and tell me about your condo. Did you move in yet?"

She held onto his hand, and turned to face him. She brushed his brown hair away from his forehead. "They finally finished painting, and I was able to sleep there last night. All the furniture is still in the middle of the rooms away from the walls, but tonight I'll be able move the pieces back to where I want them. It has a nice view of down town, and across the valley. I'd like to show it to you sometime."

"I'd enjoy seeing the place where you live. Especially at night." He laughed.

Dan's cell phone rang. "Yes, okay, good. We'll be leaving in the next few minutes to drop Jenna off at her work. Then we'll get back on the road." He listened for a moment. "Sure, I'll drive back tomorrow. Talk to you later." He dropped his phone in his pocket.

Dan faced the group "They've arrested the two perps and the girl. Tomorrow they will go to federal court for an arraignment. I think Tina will be the only one to get a bail hearing. Back on the road, gang. Let's roll." He stood and cleaned off his portion of the table.

Once they all were seated in the car, Dan turned to Rafe. "The Cottonwood police, with the help of SLC's finest, found some strong evidence against these guys, and tightened their case."

Dan drove to the mall and up into the parking garage. He stopped close to the elevators

*****

"Good bye everyone." But Jenna kissed Alistair on his cheek. "Call me when you return to Claire's."

"You be watchful, sweet girl." Alistair said.

"I will." She waved. Rafe followed Jenna and escorted her to her offices.

Chapter Twenty

When Dan and Angela dropped Alistair off at Claire's house she greeted him with a hug, and ushered him into the kitchen for a bowl of fresh vegetable soup and a toasted cheese sandwich.

"By the time I return to England I'm going to be bulging out of my clothes. I have had nothing but wonderful food since I arrived here."

"Hey if you consider soup and sandwich 'wonderful', you must have been scrounging for food in England. Besides, you are anything but 'bulging'. You and Mac irritate me sometimes, both of you are lean and have healthy appetites. I've always had to 'watch' what I eat."

"Well, I do appreciate your efforts, and when I was with Jenna, all she did was cook for me." He said.

"Speaking of Jenna, you should call her. She and I had a good chat on the phone just before you came in."

"I planned to call her later, but I'll finish my supper and ring her up right after." A very few minutes later he picked up the kitchen phone and dialed Jenna's cell phone.

"Alistair, I see you're back with Claire."

"Yes, I arrived back about a half hour ago. She had supper waiting for me, and I just finished eating." He said.

"You looked better. I suppose that means the shoulder is healing. Does it bother your much?"

"No, Claire hands me pills every morning, and every night. She and I are going to work on some simple therapy exercises tomorrow. Do you realize that tomorrow it will be seven days since I jumped into your car?"

"When do you think you'll return to England? Perhaps soon?" She asked.

"I don't know. Claire had a call from Mac this afternoon. They have arrested Howard Rutledge. He's the CEO of World Wide, but they still don't have a list of all those involved in the drug smuggling operation. Scotland Yard and Mac still don't know if there is anyone else in the company who is 'dirty' as Mac calls it. The 'Yard' in London, and the FBI here in the U. S. are going to have a video chat tomorrow."

"Since tomorrow is Friday, and I don't have to return back to work until Tuesday, I decided I could drive down tomorrow evening, and spend the weekend with you - - - - and Claire."

"You'd come down for a visit!? I'd really- - - - - -, I mean I'd be so happy to spend the New Year with you. I'm sure Claire wouldn't mind. She's lonely, and misses Mac. Please take care while driving."

"I'll check the weather report, and listen to an audio book in my car. I'll pick a good mystery. Besides I can call you on the drive down and tell you of my progress as I drive. See you tomorrow evening." Excitement came into her voice. "Oh, this is the best idea I've had in ages. See you tomorrow."

Eight-thirty p.m. Pacific Time, December 29th

Dan forester had barely walked into his Las Vegas apartment when the phone rang. As he picked it up as he shrugged out of his coat, and threw it over the couch.

The voice on the line said "Dan? Good, you've returned. to 'Vegas. This is Strickland."

"Director, how are you this evening?" Dan walked over to the refrigerator and found a can of light beer. "Yes, I barely walked in. No, the weather was no problem."

"I spoke to Inspector McIntire of Scotland Yard. We have permission to set up a three-way video conference call, between us, Salt Lake FBI, and the Police in Scotland Yard in London. We need to coordinate this investigation involving Powell, the people in London, and the local owners of *Ultimate Batteries, Corp.* We're planning to update everyone working on this case. They have new information we'll want to know, as well as inform them of what we've learned."

"Sounds like a good information exchange. When and where?" Dan asked.

"At our offices, tomorrow morning at seven- thirty A.M.. I want you to be ready to report on your investigation so far."

"Thanks for calling, sir. I'll be there with my report. Good night." Dan set the phone down. He walked to the refrigerator, and set the can back in. He would need to stay awake for the next hour or so. He rubbed his eyes, and they burned like sandpaper. The one-day trip he had just returned from had been over a twelve-hour drive. He needed to be sharp to write up his report.

It concerned Alistair and Jenna's identification of the perps. After booting up his computer, he went to the kitchen and emptied the carafe of coffee he had made early that morning. After warming it in the microwave, he winced as he tasted it. More like' road tar' than coffee, but it would keep him awake long enough to type up his paperwork.

When he finished, he flopped on his couch, kicked off his boots and shook out a pillow. Later, he woke cold, because he had not turned up the heat in his apartment. He must have forgotten to adjust the thermostat.

Staggering into his bedroom he took off his slacks and threw them over a chair, lay down on his bed and drew up the heavy quilt. With supreme effort he flipped on his alarm clock, and sunk back into an exhausted sleep.

The alarm clock sang its happy tune at exactly six- thirty A.M. the next morning. Dan groaned in agony at the sound, and pounded it to silence. He did manage to roll out of bed, and shuffle into the bathroom and the shower.

Seven- thirty A.M. Las Vegas, Eight- thirty A.M. Salt Lake, Three- thirty P.M., London. December 30th

As the rain drummed against the window of the Las Vegas offices, of the FBI, V. I. Strickland smiled, and nodded as his agents filed into the conference room. "Grab some coffee, teas, or whatever your preference and have a bagel, too. Take a seat, for we are soon to begin our video conference."

Agent Soder, their in-house video tech, had set up the video feed to a large retractable screen at one end of the room. At approximately seven- thirty A.M. the screen came to life with the Blue and White Logo of the FBI. The scene changed to the conference room in Salt Lake and focused on a man Dan did not recognize. "I'm Director Carlson, good morning, Las Vegas. We're waiting for the satellite feed from London."

The screen changed to the Logo of the British Crown, and Scotland Yard above it. There was some adjusting done and half the screen was filled with a board room, in dark wood. A man with a cheerful smile, thinning dark hair wearing a double-breasted, blue pin striped suit, filled the screen. "Greetings from your British counterparts. I'm Inspector McIntire, and I have with me, this afternoon one of your own, Dexter MacCandlass, and our Deputy James Conover. We have both Salt Lake and Las Vegas on our screen. I hope you have a similar view. As I understand it, we are to exchange information on the case that began with an attempted murder of a British citizen, Alistair Powell. Would Salt Lake please pick it up for this point?"

"Yes, I'm Director Carlson; We will present our investigation up to this point in time.. The attack on Alistair Powell was first investigated by the Cottonwood Police. Two North Korean nationals were arrested for firing an automatic weapon at an automobile, within city limits. We found out later the vehicle was registered to Jenna Barlow. Mr. Powell was a passenger in that car. The NK's were released on Monday, December 26th on a technicality, but their weapons were confiscated."

"Later in the week, the Salt Lake Crime Investigation Team

found a bullet in a pillar of the parking garage where Powell had been attacked. The bullet came from one of the weapons the Cottonwood police had confiscated. Mr. Powell's cellular phone was also found."

"On December 27th, an attempted kidnapping of Ms. Barlow, in the same parking garage, was thwarted by three of our FBI agents. The perps were arrested. Yesterday Ms. Barlow identified them in a lineup. Mr. Powell also identified one of them as his alleged attacker."

"Two FBI agents went to the *Ultimate Batteries, Corp.* operating in a rented warehouse in Provo, Utah. After some investigation, they arrested Tina Woo, who worked there. After examination of her personal computer, we found that she was in contact with one of perps arrested. We also found several emails sent to North Korea. One of the men arrested for trying to kidnap Ms. Barlow is Chin Wah. We believe he is also in the country illegally. He had falsified documents and was attending the university in Provo."

"Quite interesting, crucial formation." McIntire said.

"On our side of the 'pond' we have arrested Howard Rutledge, CEO of *World Wide Electronics. Limited.* Also located was a lorry, originated from a warehouse owned by Rutledge. The cargo on it was destined for a ship at the Liverpool docks. The truck had been, as you Yanks say, hi-jacked. Two men, drivers of the truck were murdered. They and the truck were found at a location near the sea, where a landing strip had been built. We surmise that this place was used by the NK's to snuggle in their drugs. We believe the shipment went into an aircraft, which could be as large as a B737."

"We have also arrested two blokes who tried to break into MacCandlass' hotel room with the intent of murder. Mac, here subdued the both of them." McIntire moved to put a hand on Mac's shoulder.

"Attempted murder!? Hey Mac, you've been busy over there." Dan's mouth twitched.

"Now gentlemen." The inspector said. "What are your thoughts as to how the investigation should move from this point?"

"We're still thin on a motive." Balfour said. "The disc everyone was willing to kill for has been found to be incomplete."

"We're wondering if the bad guys knew this?" Carlson commented.

"There has to be an overriding motive. What is it?" Dan asked.

"That has been bothering me, too." Mac said.

"Originally, the NK's were making money selling drugs to Rutledge, as well as, I'm sure to others who would deal them. Then the NK's wanted something more from Rutledge. And he sent Powell to Utah to get a copy of the specs for these extended life batteries. Do they want to manufacture them, or just one specific size? They couldn't wait until Powell returned to England, but had to go after the disc in Salt Lake. Why?" Mac said.

"At first, I thought it was to steal the technology from the battery manufactures. Now my thoughts are along the same road as MacCandlass, here." McIntire said.

"And because of our knowledge of that nation's behavior is in the world, this whole situation makes me even more nervous." Strickland said.

Chapter Twenty-One

At that moment, an aide walked into the video feed from Los Vegas, and handed a note to Director Strickland. He scanned it quickly, and glanced up at the camera. "Gentlemen, we now have a situation in in Tehran, Iran. One of our satellite feeds just picked up a plane with markings from African Emirates. It landed at a small airfield near Tehran last evening for refueling. The plane took off early this morning heading east. Apparently, the plane left without international registration. From the satellite feed the plane was parked overnight inside a hanger. We have no idea if the manifest was checked. It possibly could have been carrying illegal contraband and false papers.

Our satellite then' picked it up' when it took off from the small airfield in Iran. The U. S Air Craft Carrier *Robert Jamison,* picked it up on its RADAR and they are tracking it. They are investigating." Strickland said.

"That could be the plane that took off from the air strip near Liverpool." Mac said.

"A plane? How large?" Dan asked. "What's the cargo?"

"As large as a B737. At least some of the cargo was gourmet food, and spirits." Mac said.

Carlson cleared his throat. "Gentlemen, let's get back to the original puzzle. What did they want from the battery company and what model?"

"Why don't we send one or two computers from World Wide, and deliver them to the Battery manufactures in Provo, and have their people construct a battery for it."

"What type of computer?" Mac asked.

"A small one, notebook size." Dan said.

"What are you thinking, Daniel my lad?" McIntire asked.

"Are you thinking of a computer that could be used as a trigger, armed with a remote mechanism?" Mac asked.

McIntire nodded. "Precisely."

"Who would know, or suspect that companies like *World Wide* and *Ultimate Batteries* could construct such a prototype?" Higby asked.

"Alistair Powell. We'll ring him up and speak with him." The inspector said.

"Possibly they wanted not just the disc, but also Alistair Powell, too. Trying to kidnap Jenna Barlow would give them a bargaining chip if they wanted Alistair. Where is he now?" Inspector McIntire asked.

"He's here in St. George, Utah and could begin work at their warehouse in Provo, with Jamison and Reacher." Johnson said.

"I could deliver the notebooks, and help Alistair." Mac said.

"Gentlemen, I think we have a workable plan. We should contact Ultimate Batteries. Mac needs to return to the U.S and soon as possible."

"I will make a visit to the factory at *Ultimate Batteries* this very afternoon." Higby said.

"I believe we have a plan and the people to put into action. It was a pleasure speaking with all of you." Good afternoon." McIntire said. The screen from London went blank.

December 30, ten a.m. Mountain time, Rawley, Utah

When Alistair picked up the phone, he nearly dropped it. It was an exchange from London.

"Hi Al, it's Mac. How are you doing?"

"Mac, how good it is to speak with you. How are you enjoying the English winter? Oh, I'm sorry Claire has already left for the clinic."

"I figured she wouldn't be home. It's you I planned to talk with. I need to ask you some questions. Rather, it is Inspector McIntire who wants to question you." Alistair heard a low voice and then another line pick up.

"Good afternoon, Inspector McIntire, Scotland Yard, here. We've made some progress regarding your case, the attack on your person, occurring there in America."

"Inspector, it's so good of you to be interested in my personal situation." Alistair was at a loss for more words.

"Do you think you could you work with those young men at *Ultimate Batteries*? We, Scotland Yard and the American FBI want you to build a prototype; Combining one of your computers with a suitable battery that they could design. You would be working with a small computer. When MacCandlass returns, he will be bringing you two models."

"A small one sir? I believe they could build a battery to fit such a particular computer." Alistair said.

"Good. I'm putting MacCandlass on a flight to America tomorrow morning. He will be carrying the models. I've already spoken to your man Carruthers, as to the two computers he will want delivered to you. You may call your man. Do you remember the number?"

"Yes sir, but I would have to use the land line here in St. George."

"I know, however we are sending a cellular phone for you with Mac. You may continue to use the land line until Mac puts the new one in your hands. Oh, I've called your family in York and told them you are recovering from an accident, and you'll be able to call them." McIntire said.

"Of course, I must call my family." Alistair had been so involved with everything else that had happened, his family had slipped from his mind. "They must be very worried."

*****

Mac picked up the line. "Hey, Al, how's your shoulder? We've decided that you need to see a regular MD. Claire has one in mind; she'll set an appointment for you. I'll be seeing you, probably on New

128

Year's Day. When we get together, I'll explain all that has transpired in this 'caper' of ours. Take it easy. See you in a couple of days." The line went dead.

Alistair's mind was in a jumble. What should he do first? Call his family in York, and assure them he was fine and would be staying in the States for another week, perhaps longer?

While working at *Ultimate Batteries*, where would he stay, in a motel? How far was Jenna's condo from the warehouse in West Provo? That's where he wanted to be, with her. But would she want him there, living with her, sharing her living arrangements, her bed? He should to wait until the right moment to ask her.

*****

Claire came dancing into the kitchen about lunchtime. When Alistair came out of the den, she was all smiles. "Al, when is Jenna supposed to arrive here?"

"This evening. She said around ten, depending on when she could leave her work. She said she would call during her travels." He couldn't diminish the grin on his face.

Claire gave a delighted laugh. "It looks like both of us have something to smile about. Mac called me. He's flying home tomorrow. He'll be landing at Salt Lake International about seven tomorrow evening. So- - -- - I booked a hotel room at the Marriot in Salt Lake for tomorrow night. I wouldn't want Mac or me to be forced to drive home that late at night. A night in a hotel will be good for both of us." She widened her eyes in mock innocence, but then she began to laugh. "If I leave right after lunch tomorrow, I'll make to Salt Lake City by five or so."

"A little reunion: Sound's lovely, and I'm sure both of you will enjoy it. The Sheraton has a good restaurant. You may want to try it." He tilted his head and smiled. "When do you think you'll return?"

"Sunday evening, sometime. It depends on how late we sleep,

and which football bowl game is on, and when.”

“Bowl game?” Your football teams play in bowl?” He clapped his hand over his mouth, but then he smiled. “You’re speaking of the shape of stadium, are you not?”

She frowned. “I suppose that’s how they decided to call these bowl games in the beginning. It’s much more complicated than that. You’ll have to have Mac explain the finer points of how the teams manage to be invited to play in all the end-of season games.”

“All of this means that Jenna and I will have the house to ourselves tomorrow night.” He couldn’t suppress a big smile, but then he decided to change the subject. “I had a phone call, too. Mac is bringing along some small computers from our factory. I’m supposed to work with Jamison and Reacher at *Ultimate Batteries* to build a prototype.”

“Mac mentioned something about that. First, however, you need to see a real physician. I called an older doctor, a friend of my father’s. He’s expecting us within the hour.” She turned and began pulling sandwich makings from the refrigerator. As she talked, she began making two tuna and cheese sandwiches and grabbed two cans of soda from the refrigerator. As she worked, she talked over her shoulder.

“I’m taking you to a Dr. Fetzer. He’s semi-retired. He was nice enough to see you on short notice. “Here.” She set a plate on the table, holding a sandwich and potato chips, along with the soda and glass with ice in it. “Eat. We need to go soon.” She walked out of the room.

“Aren’t you going to eat, too?” He glanced at her lunch still resting on the kitchen counter.

“I’m just going to the bathroom. This is what I do all day.” She mumbled.

*****

Claire drove east towards St. George, and turned down an older street to an attractive red brick house with white shutters. She parked in the driveway and climbed out of her car. "Come on, he has an office in his house."

They were greeted by a lean, gray-haired man in his late sixties. "Claire, how are you? It's so good to see you." He gave her a hug. "This must be Mr. Powell. Would you follow me to my examining room?"

Alistair glanced back at Claire, but she already had taken a seat on a small sofa. He followed the doctor down a hall, and into the typical medical examining room.

"Sit up here, after you take off all clothing above the waist." The doctor gestured to an examining table. "Oh, by the way, I'm Dr. Fetzer."

Alistair did the doctor's bidding, shivering a little from the change in temperature. This room was cooler than Claire's warm house.

The doctor slipped on a pair of latex gloves, and carefully probed the healing wound in Alistair's shoulder. He checked both the entrance and exit sites." Now, flex your shoulder. Can you extend your arm forward?"

Alistair winced, but could do ask the doctor asked.

"Ah, some pain, right?" Fetzer asked. "Can you raise your arm? Good. Now, put your arm out and turn your palm. Turn it back. Now bend your elbow and lift your arm as high as you can. I can see the strain on your face. Sit quietly for a moment." He took Alistair's blood pressure and listened to his heart. "What is your age? As Alistair answered, he wrote it down on a chart. "Let's measure you. Take off your shoes and come stand on the scale."

Alistair went to the scale, and with a horizontal metal measure, the doctor measured his height and weighed him.

"Six foot one and a half in height. One hundred eight-two pounds. Good weight for your height. And 36 years old, you're in your prime. Make good use of your years. When you are living in England, what do you do for exercise?"

"I used to be on a rowing team, but my job interfered. My company has a gymnasium area, and I run on good days."

"You are a fortunate man. That bullet could have done much more damage. Those two women did a good job of treating and caring for you. Now I want you to go through those exercises you did, each day about five times, and as you become more comfortable, up the number each day. Claire said she gave you some antibiotics, correct?"

"Yes, I'm still taking them. I started Sunday evening. She gave me enough pills to last ten days."

"Put your clothes back on. Each day you immobilize an area of the body, you lose two percent of the muscle mass in the same area. So now you must slowly build it back. I'll give Claire some samples for you. Take care of yourself." He patted Alistair on his other shoulder, and walked out of the room.

CHAPTER TWENTY-TWO

The only thing Alistair could find to do was to watch the Tele or TV as the American's called it, He found some game shows then switched channels to a family situation comedy. After a few minutes he jumped and began to pace, and check the clock.

Claire went upstairs to pack for her trip to Salt Lake.

A little after nine P.M. he did find a mystery show he found interesting, but in the middle of it, he heard the now familiar crunch of car tires on the gravel in the side driveway. He walked swiftly to the kitchen door. When he snapped on the porch light, he was relieved to see the silver Lexus.

Claire was right behind him. She must have seen the car pull in from her bedroom window. Jenna exited the car and came around to the door.

"Hi Al. " She flashed him a smile. As she pushed her way into the house, he wrapped his right arm around her and pulled her inside. She hugged him, and he kissed her.

Claire stood back waiting for the two of them to disengage themselves. "Let's get your things in, Jenna, because it's cold out there."

Jenna dragged in an overnight bag, her purse, and laptop. Alistair carried in a sack of food she had brought.

"How was your drive down?" Claire asked.

"I was fighting a south wind. That means a storm is coming." She answered.

"I was planning to drive to SLC tomorrow to pick up Mac." Claire frowned. "We'd better check the ten o'clock newscast. See what the weather guy has to say." The three of them settled into the den, to watch the TV. The ten P.M. news came on and they were forced to watch and listen to the first eighteen minutes of news before the weather report.

The weather reporter from the Salt Lake CBS affiliate began his TV segment.

"A cold front is on our 'doorstep', and should begin entering the state tomorrow late morning. It will affect the northern part of the state by afternoon tomorrow, but The Salt Lake Metro area will not get any precipitation until evening. That means if you are out and about on New Year's Eve, driving may become hazardous. Please be careful, and if you choose to celebrate too much, plan for a designated driver, or call a cab."

"Claire, if you leave early enough, you'll get to the city before the storm really hits. Take it easy, there is going to heavy traffic." Jenna said.

"I'll call one of my part- time girls to close the clinic tomorrow at around two p.m. I'll try to leave by ten in the morning. Right now, I need you two to vacate the sofa, so I can make up a bed for Jenna. Alistair, go find some ice cream. We'll make some sundaes."

"Jenna, would you like some ice cream?" Alistair asked.

"Yes, I think so." She yawned. 'There's serotonin in ice scream. It will help me to sleep."

"Is that why we like to eat it, or drink milk late a night?" He asked.

"That's the theory, anyway, or the excuse to eat it." Claire went to the cupboard and found three suitable bowls, while Alistair searched the freezer for vanilla ice cream, and he found two flavors: Chocolate chip and vanilla.

When Claire finished the sundaes, Jenna came into the kitchen. "Oh, they look good enough to eat." They sat down to enjoy their treat. Jenna stifled another yawn and rubbed her eyes.

"You're tired, girl. Your bed is all ready for you." Claire said.

"I've been up since before six A.M." She stood and set her ice cream bowl in the sink. "Thanks, I'm going to bed." She hugged Claire and walked to the hall bathroom and closed the door.

"I think I'll say good night, too." Claire followed Jenna out of the kitchen, and went upstairs.

Alistair continued sitting at the table, stirring his now melted ice cream. Should he go to bed, or wait for Jenna to come out of the bathroom? He was a mixture of shyness and need. He stood by the bathroom door and finally lifted his hand to knock. He barely touched the door, before it flew open.

"Oh, Al- - - - I thought, -- - - - - -ah?"

"You thought I would be Claire. Sorry, It's only me. I wanted to wish you good night."

Her smile made his heart beat hard and fast. 'How's this?' She rose up on tip toe and kissed him. Her mouth was warm, soft and her lips parted for the tip of his tongue.

He backed her into the small bathroom and closed the door. The kisses became hungry, and he pulled her hard against him. He could feel her breasts against his chest. His hand went down her back, and he could feel the indentation of her waistline and stroked the curve of her hip.

She broke the kiss and put her arms around his neck and gazed into his eyes. "Let's save this 'heat' for tomorrow, because when we're alone, we can explore- - - - -, all the possibilities."

He slid away from her. "Yes, I so want to make love to you, but not this furtive groping. I can wait until we have all the time we need to explore each other in a warm, comfortable bed."

"Thank you for understanding. I'm not terribly experienced at all this. You may be disappointed."

"I doubt it." He took a deep breath and opened the door; "Until tomorrow." He kissed her forehead and turned to walk slowly upstairs.

After tossing and turning most of the night, Alistair finally managed to sleep. His mind was working overtime, going from knowing Jenna was just down stairs and wanting her, to trying to understand the events of the past week.

When he did wake, shower and dress, the scent of coffee and bacon teased his nose. One of the girls must be cooking breakfast. He found Jenna standing by the stove. He wrapped his arms around here and planted a kiss on her neck.

She must have heard or felt his presence before he touched her, because she turned in his arms, looked up at him, and giggled. "Morning Al, you slept late. It's after nine A.M.

He glanced at the black and white clock hanging on the wall by the table. "My word, I did sleep in. Has Claire already left for the clinic?"

"Yes, I heard her, woke and got up. I made her some breakfast while she packed a lunch to take in the car. Now sit down. I have a plate of breakfast for you." She lifted a foil cover on a plate and placed it in the microwave.

"Do you cook breakfast every morning?" He widened his eyes in amazement.

"Heavens no," She laughed. "Not when I have to be to work early every morning. This morning, however is special. It's a Saturday, New Year's Eve, and- - - - - - I have you here to further impress you with my culinary skills. Right now, I'm going to clean up the den so we can use the sofa later, to do- - - - - - - -, whatever we choose to do on it." As she walked away, she tossed a flirtatious glance over her shoulder.

He watched her move down the hall, vivacious, sweet, and sexy, all in one trim, blonde, blue-eyed package. He was totally smitten, and he knew it.

*****

A few minutes later she called "Al, do you want to watch a football game? The Fiesta Bowl is on. It just started."

"That sounds interesting. I'll be right there."

She had tidied up the room, and closed the drapes to block out the morning light. There was a comfortable place on the sofa for both of them. He wondered if he would like this game of American football, because he had never seen a game before. He's seen movies with a football theme, but they weren't actual games.

The flat screen TV showed a large stadium, filled with cheering spectators. The camera moved to give a view of the two teams running out from respective sidelines on to the field. The crowd cheered. Areas of the stands were filled with people dressed in the colors of their favorite team. They had placards, and signs on poles either cheering on their team, or waving negative slogans about the opposing team.

In many ways the energy and excitement reminded him of soccer games in England, but the players were dressed in uniforms that reminded him of space suits, although very colorful. They wore elaborate helmets with face guards. The rest of their bodies were covered with the bright colored jerseys and pants in their team colors with heavy padding underneath. Their shoes were equipped to run on grass or artificial turf that resembled the natural material. Many of them even wore gloves. The two teams, green on one side of the field and orange and black on the other, were several meters away from each other.

A referee wearing a black and white striped shirt set a football in the middle of the field. Both teams bent over and faced each other. One of the team members on the orange and black team kicked the ball high into the air toward the opposite team. Then both teams ran toward each other. One of the players on the green team caught the ball, and his whole team ran toward the other group. Then they all began grabbing and pushing, and falling down on the turf in big piles. One of the men on the green team, underneath everyone else, held up the football. He jumped up, tossed it to a referee. The referee put the ball on the ground at a certain spot.

The announcer said it was on the 27th yard line, and each team lined up again facing each other in certain formations. The green team had the ball, and an extremely large man tossed the ball to a smaller man behind him. That man ran backward a few steps, and threw it to another of his teammates down the field. An opposing man in black and orange jumped on the ball catcher, and threw him to the ground. Yet, when the referee blew a whistle, the jumper helped the opposing man up, and the two teams lined up again, at another place on the field. Then as they lined up, a green team player somehow got the ball, and ran down the field right to group of players from the other team. They all jumped on each other. The program suddenly changed to a commercial.

Alistair, frowning turned to Jenna. "Do you understand this game?"

Jenna turned to him and laughed. "Somewhat. The object of the game is to score a touchdown. This happens when a man tries to get the ball into the opposite end zone; Either by catching the ball or carrying it there. That gives the team six points. After that, a special man will try to kick the ball between those posts at the end of the field. If he can do that, then the team adds another point to their score."

The game came back on, and the team holding the football, was again moving toward the other team. Again, a man is pulled down, and several men from both teams grab and or fall on each other.

"Let's watch it for a few more minutes." She shook her head and laughed. "If it's too confusing, I'll search for another program. We have 150 channels to choose from."

CHAPTER TWENTY-THREE

Jenna turned her attention to Claire's desk. "Hey, there's the TV Guide. I'll find something else to watch." She thumbed through the magazine, but soon looked up and grinned. "Did you ever chance to see the film: *Avatar?*"

"No, many people at the factory viewed it and, raved that it was wonderful. Nut I never managed to make it to a theatre to see it."

She glanced down at the TV Guide again. "It's going to be on in ten minutes. You want to watch it?"

"Yes, that would be great." He grinned.

"Okay, but I have to make popcorn." She grinned.

"Popcorn, we just had breakfast." He shook his head in wonder at her.

"Can't watch a good movie without popcorn. I'll be right back." She jumped up and ran to the kitchen. She soon returned with a large bowl of popcorn and two glasses filled with ice, and two cans of soda. She plopped it all on the coffee table.

He laughed and hugged her. "You are amazing, and irrepressible." He took a large handful of popcorn. "Mmm, quite good."

The film soon started and they settled in to enjoy a super, rather incredible film.

As the closing credits rolled, Alistair looked over at Jenna, and she was half asleep. "Did you fall asleep during the film?" He couldn't believe anyone would want to miss a single frame if it.

"I guess. I haven't totally caught up on my sleep this week. You have to admit it's been rather unusual, to say the least. I suppose I need a nap."

"I understand. Can you fall asleep on this sofa?" He asked.

In answer, she curled up with a soft cushion under her head, and pulled the blanket- throw up over her. She took a deep breath and closed her eyes.

"All right. I'll leave you to rest." He was tired too, but he was not in the habit of napping. He pulled on his heavy coat, checked for some gloves in his pocket, and walked out the back door. He turned west, to a section of this little town he'd not seen before.

*****

It was raining when Alastair returned to Mac and Claire's house. His hair was damp, his shoes were wet, and his feet were cold. Jenna was at the stove stirring something in a saucepan.

She turned around as he came in. "Look at you. You're all wet. Here, let me help you out of the coat."

"What are you warming? It smells good." His stomach growled.

"Some leftover soup I found in the fridge. We can have a little snack lunch, before I take you for a drive." She reached for bowls and plates.

"Where are you taking me?" He hung his coat on a rack in the entrance way. If you don't mind, I'll run upstairs and change my shoes." He returned quickly and sat down. "Where are we going?"

"I thought since we are both here, together, in the area, I'd drive over to River Mesa. I'd like show you where I grew up."

"You want to go over to the polygamous colony?" He frowned.

She turned her head and blinked. Jenna's face was serious and a little sad.. "I've never had the courage to go even go near the town, but with you along, I- - - - -, well, I wanted you to see what I described."

"My presence has given you courage?" He sat back, and gazed at her. "That pleases me, and gives me the idea that I'm important to you. Yes, of course we should go. How far is it?"

"From here, about fifty-five miles. We can make it there in close to an hour. I don't know what reception we'll find, but at least you'll see the layout of the town."

The rain had let up, and a few heavy clouds lifted somewhat, but it still hung dark in the western sky. The road took them through St. George, then north and east to the town of Hurricane. Jenna drove up a circular road to a higher elevation. They were still driving through desert, but it was cooler, and the plant growth seemed richer. Alistair could see a farm here and there, with fields lying fallow for the winter season.

Jenna found an easy listening radio station, but the closer they came to their destination the more quiet she became. They drove past a cement factory on the west side, a shabby, empty motel on the east next a convenience store on the west of the highway, and a car repair shop, and they passed a marker reading: <u>RIVER MESA,</u>

She turned up a black top covered street with various types houses on it, but soon the pavement ended and the roadbed became hardened dirt. They passed houses that were smaller and seemed more shabby. A few of the dwellings were not completely finished, because some would lack brick overlay, or some lacked siding in places. Another house had a place where a porch should have been there but was not completed. The yards were neglected near many of them.

She turned to the north, and slowed, then stopped the car. "This is the house where I grew up." She pointed to her left at a two story, gray block house. It was set back from the road and had a partial sloping lawn.

There was no movement, no one stirred from the houses. No children were out walking. Because of the rain and remaining clouds, the whole town had a dark, gloomy neglected aspect.

Suddenly an older Chevy Blazer pulled up next to them in a splash of wet dirt. A large, fair-haired man rolled down the front passenger window and yelled. "What are you lookin' fer?"

Jenna rolled down her window. "I was looking at that house. I'm not planning to bother anyone."

"Well, yer trespassin'. So, it's my job to escort you to the main road. I'm gonna follow you out of town. Ya get it?"

Jenna shook her head, and let out a large sigh. "Okay, I'm going." She slowly drove back the same route she had come in. When she reached the edge of the highway, she stopped the car and surprised

Alistair by climbing out of the automobile. She stood quietly near her door. The man in the Blazer behind her did the same. She looked up at the big man and said, "Aren't you Clinton Bybee?"

"Might be, what's it to you?" He had such a scowl, that Alistair reacted by getting out of the car and moving to Jenna's side.

"I was two years behind you at middle school. "I'm Jenna Barlow."

Clinton stared down at Jenna for a long moment. "Well, I'll be- - - -. Where you been all these years? Did ya end up in Vegas?" He sneered.

She shook her head. "I went to St. George, and finished high school there. "Then I- - - -.

But he cut her off. "This is a pretty nice car yer drivin'. Did yer man, here buy it for ya?"

Alistair was hot with anger at this uncouth creature. "No, she graduated college, found a good job and bought it herself!"

"You a foreigner? Where you from?" He turned to Alistair with a black scowl.

"Yes, I'm from the UK, here working with the FBI on a case."

"UK? That in Europe someplace? FBI huh. Good luck working with this gov-ment." He shifted his gaze to Jenna. "So, Jenna, you want to leave the evil world behind, and come back here un live with us Godfearin' people?" He appraised her with a long, full body gaze. "Get away from the lyin' gov-ment? If ya do, email me, and I'd be willin' to take ya as a wife." He flashed a lascivious grin. "Ya seemed to grow up pretty good, and yer hair's long."

Jenna shivered, and backed away. She glanced at Alistair. "Let's go, Al, I've seen enough." She slid into the car, started the engine and turned to the north, before Al even had the car door shut.

*****

"Thank you for the educational tour. I would have never believed what you told me without seeing it myself. That certainly was an unpleasant bloke." Jenna's hands were trembling on the steering wheel. "Are you alright?' He asked.

She roared up the road another mile or so, but then abruptly pulled over and stopped the car. She dropped her head on the steering wheel, and began to sob.

He patted her, rubbed her back, and waited until she stopped crying.

"Can you find me a tissue? She choked. "Look on your side of the seat, in the door pocket."

He fished out a fist full of tissues and pushed them into her hand. "I could drive, if you trust me to do so. I rented a car and drove it back and- - - - - -! I wonder what happened to my car rental?"

"You had a rented car? Of course you did. I wonder if it is still in the parking garage." She laughed through her tears. "Thanks for changing the subject. Oh Al, I escaped! Can you believe that jerk? Take me as a wife? Not in this lifetime." She slapped the steering wheel and growled. She reached over and tilted Alistair's face to hers and kissed him. "Thank you for coming with me. I really needed to slam shut my mental door on that town, that part of my life, that weird religion."

"I'll go back with you again if you keep kissing me like that." He took a deep breath, shaky from experiencing this town.

She put the car in gear, and drove north. Each mile she drove took her to St. George, and returned her to the life she had hammered out for herself this past fifteen years. Perhaps, now she could have a normal, loving relationship with Alistair.

As Jenna passed the eight-mile mark to St George, Alistair turned to her. "You and Claire have been preparing meals for me for eight days. "It's my turn to feed you. I can now use my credit cards. Where is a good restaurant?"

"If we can find one, we can actually get into. It *is* New Year's Eve. Every eating establishment is going to be packed with people." She turned to him and touched his arm. "I appreciate the gesture. We'll go see what we can find."

They drove south on Telegraph Road and passed The *Texas Road House*. The parking lot was full, and people had parked in other areas and were walking over to the restaurant. Next, they cruised by *Olive Garden, Chili's, Red Lobster* even the Sport's Bar.

"I have an idea." Jenna turned the car around and drove north for half a block. "How about a serve yourself, all you can eat place. If we can find a parking place, we may get a table in there."

"*Chuck-a-Rama?* What is that place?" He asked as he sounded out the words on the sign.

"That, my English guest, is where we're going." She smiled, turned left and maneuvered the Lexis into a newly vacated parking spot. They climbed out, and walked across the rain spattered concrete.

Chapter Twenty-Four

They pushed open the door, where a crowded line of humanity was waiting to be seated. There were families with several children, senior citizens, young adults hanging onto each other as if they were on a ship tilting into the sea.

Alistair's eyes took it all in, and could not associate this place with anything in his mother country. After about ten minutes of watching children climbing on the railing, separating the rows of humanity, or hanging onto their parents, and yelling "How much longer, Dad?"

Alistair and Jenna reached the pay-first desk. The girl at the desk was amazingly cheerful. "How many, sir?" She asked with a smile.

"Two of us." He motioned at Jenna. She tilted her head at the girl, and smiled. "Will you take my Visa?" Alistair produced the card, and slid it across the desk top.

"Yes, sir." She ran it through the reader, and produced a bill for him to sign. "Now wait at the end of this line, here. A girl will seat you." She waved at a place behind a family of six.

They finally managed to be seated in a booth. Jenna tossed her coat on the bench. "Put the bill on the table, take off your coat and leave it on the seat, and we're off to start our grazing." Jenna grinned, and she did what she had told him to do.

She took him first to the salad table, an oblong affair loaded with all kinds of greens and other fresh salad ingredients. She handed him a plate, picked a plate for herself and began to assemble a salad.

He watched her, and did much the same. There was a huge variety from which to choose, as well as other salad toppings and dressings. The place was crowded, body to body with all sizes and shapes of people.

Jenna deftly dodged them, as she scooped up table ware, and napkins from a center table. She carried her heavily laden plate to their booth. Almost immediately a young girl, he presumed to be of college age, asked what they would like as a beverage.

"Do you have tea?" Alistair asked.

"Iced tea, sure. There's also coffee, sodas and fruit juice, too."

Alistair frowned. "All right, I'll take iced tea."

"Make it two." Jenna said. "Thanks. Oops, I forgot something." She slid out of the booth, and returned momentarily with a plate of wheat rolls and a slab of cinnamon butter.

The rolls were large and fluffy, and a good accompaniment to the salad. The food was fresh and of good quality. He checked the total of the charge on his credit slip. This was amazing. The two of them were having what seemed to be fresh, well-prepared food, the customer's choice as to quantity, all for a little more than thirty dollars. One did need to ignore the noise from children and babies.

As he finished the salad, he said. "Do we fetch another plate and choose the main course?"

"Yep, follow me." Jenna grinned.

There were tables of hot food, roast prime rib, ham, or turkey, vegetables, and more breads.. A young man stood waiting for you make a choice, and he would carve a slice from a roast for you. Alistair found potatoes, gravy, vegetables, and fresh fruit. The main problem was to not step on a small child, or bump into a large individual carrying an overflowing plate All the while fighting to get back to their booth. "This certainly is a new experience for me." He said, as he scooped up a forkful of mashed potatoes.

"It usually isn't this crowded, but it is a Holiday, and people are out and about. On a Sunday afternoon, it can get like this." She took a bite of chicken. She smiled and shrugged. "I thought you might enjoy an experience of eating at a restaurant quite popular in Utah."

"Is this the only one? How did this place come to be?"

"I believe the first one opened close to downtown Salt Lake, possibly 40 years ago." A man had a vision of an all-you-can-eat restaurant. So, he opened one.

His daughter married a man who wanted to improve and franchise the unique idea. For years there was just two or three of them. Then the husband's family got involved, and now his sons and his daughter run them. There have been some locations that have closed, but more have opened, redecorated and refined."

"Is there one close to your condo in Salt Lake?" He asked.

"I believe so. Perhaps, less than five miles away. Why do you want to come up and dine with me there?" She chuckled.

He raised his eyebrows. "Possibly, who knows?" He began to earnestly attack his plate of food.

*****

In the dark of the last evening in December, they drove back to Rawley, and settled down in the den. Neither one was interested in watching another football game, or even the movie Jenna had found. The phone rang, and Jenna jumped up to answer it.

"Hello. Claire, how are you?"

"Did you find something or somewhere to eat?" Claire asked.

"Yes, I took Alistair to *Chuck-a-Rama*" Jenna said laughter in her voice.

"I'll bet that was an unusual experience for him. I'd like to hear his version of it, sometime."

"How's Mac? Did he arrive in Salt Lake safely?"

"Yes, he's tired, but he's now taking a shower. That should revive him for a few hours. It's going to snow up here. I'll let you know if that slows our return trip. Meanwhile, how are you and Alistair doing?"

"We're fine. I you want to know if I'm planning to sleep with him, the answer *is* yes. Whether we do more than sleep, is still the big question. I'll let you know tomorrow."

Claire cleared her throat. "Nothing like being candid, girl. Whatever you do, all I can say is enjoy. I've learned Al's a real sweetheart. There aren't many like him out there. Keep those thoughts in mind." Claire laughed. "We'll call you, if and when we get on the road. Oh, one more thing. Mac had a call, concerning Alistair's car rental. The company came and found it in the parking garage, with Christmas gifts still in it.

The Salt Lake police informed the rental company that Alistair had been shot in the parking garage, and the attempt on his life was part of an FBI investigation. Mac and Alistair need to call the car rental company, but the Feds want only certain information to be released."

"Okay, I'll tell him. Have a Merry, Happy New Year, I certainly plan to enjoy, the end of this and the beginning of the New Year coming tomorrow. See ya when you make home. Bye"

When Jenna ended her phone call, Alistair decided to call his family in York. To wish them a Happy New Year, and reassure them that he was healing well. After he ended the call, he could hear Jenna in the small bath next to the den, and decided to go upstairs and take a shower. He wanted to be appealing to Jenna for he planned on a night of lovemaking.

When he came into the bedroom he occupied, he found her propped up, in his bed. "Jenna- - - -, I didn't expect, I mean- -- - - -." He stopped. "Seeing you here is a pleasant surprise. Welcome to my bed."

Her smile seemed a bit coy, but then she slid out of bed, to reveal a pink and white striped night shirt with sleeves past her elbows. The gown, however, barely grazed her knees.

"Pajamas? I didn't take you for a guy who would sleep in them. I do like the plaid bottoms, and the knitted top. It will easily slip off over your head."

"My apartment in England is chilly in the winter. When I knew I was coming to the Rocky Mountains, I - - - - - -." She stopped his explanation by wrapping her arms around his neck, and on tip toe, kissed him.

His heart thumped with joy; because she wanted to stay the night with him. They stood kissing, and he slid his hand through the silken stands of her hair. Backing her against the bed, they fell onto the mattress.

She rolled over to the far side of the bed, and held open the covers inviting him to come in. He moved close to her and began an exploration of her body. She matched his ardor kiss for kiss, caress for caress. He straddled her, on knees and outstretched arms. As he bent down to kiss her again, his left arm collapsed, and he was forced to roll away from her.

"Augh, bloody shoulder!" He gripped his upper arm as if that would take away the intense pain, but then he threw his right arm across his face.

*****

She came up on one elbow. "Your shoulder? I wondered if it was strong enough for this rather intense activity." She stroked his face, wrapped her arm across his chest, and settled down near his right shoulder. Suddenly, she sat up. "Oh, I just remembered you need to take your meds."

He glanced up at her in the soft light from the hallway, his eyes wide. "I wanted to be the consummate lover, and bring you marvelous pleasure, and you're thinking about my medications?" He watched her break into a giggle.

"Al, I'm sorry, but my mind sometimes is a little twisted." Yet she smiled down at him. "I'll be right back." She shot out the door, and he could hear her bouncing down the stairs. He pushed up on his right shoulder and shook his head.

He could hear her rummaging around in the kitchen. What an introduction to a night of love?

She soon returned with a tray, two glasses, a plate of chocolate cookies, two pills, on a napkin and a carton of milk. From the nightstand she poured him a glass of milk. "Take your pills first." She climbed back into bed with the cookies. "I was about to say that there are several ways or positions to make love."

He laughed. "You sound like a bloody sex manual."

"That is probably where I've picked up my knowledge of intimacy." She opened her hands, and held a cookie.

"Are you telling me you're still a virgin? I worried about that probability."

"No, but I haven't much experience. Only with one guy, and he was as 'green' about sex as I was." She said between bites of the cookie.

"Our first hurdle was finding a private place to get together. He was a native of St. George, and a really sweet guy, but quite dominated by his mother. One weekend his parents went out of town, and he called me. I managed to get the afternoon off, because I was working at a coffee shop at the time." She sipped her milk.

"We went in his room, with all his boyhood collections here and there. And on his single bed, we managed to 'deflower' each other, but it wasn't very exciting. Yet for me it was the ultimate rebellion against what I had been taught, brainwashed actually, my whole, young life."

Chapter Twenty-Five

"I remembered a special meeting with the 'prophet', the guy who is now serving a life sentence in Texas for child abuse. Anyway, the man cautioned, that we were to have no physical contact with the boys our age or those of teen age. No touching, hand holding, anything, for this was against God's commandments. We were to be virgin brides for our husbands when were chosen to be 'spiritual' wives. We were to be pure as a new born babe. But in the next breath he began to tell us how to bring our husband to ecstasy. How to touch and tease and pleasure him. What men liked, etc."

"How old were you when you were forced to listen to his preaching? And was that the extent of your sexual education?" He asked, sitting up in bed with her shoulder to shoulder.

"Just about. I believe I was possibility twelve or thirteen years old. Since I didn't hang around long enough to become a spiritual wife, and my mother had passed on, I didn't get the bride lecture from her, or anyone else. When Fern and I lived at our foster mother's house, I took a course in human physiology at the high school. I spent many hours on the internet reading up on sexual anatomy of both girls and guys. It was very enlightening."

"Did you and this boy go on with your sexual experimentation?" He asked, and picked up her hand and stroked her fingers.

"We had a few more clandestine meetings, but there was no real spark between us. Later he met a girl he liked, and dated her later of that year. Actually, Joel and I became good friends." She sighed.

"How old were you." He asked.

"Nineteen: A freshman in college." She sat up and faced him, and passed him the plate of cookies.

"Are these the same cookies that Claire brought to the cottage?" He asked.

"Yes, I brought them down yesterday. Aren't they the best?'

"I'll say one thing. This is a new experience for me. I plan to make love to you and instead we sit in bed eating cookies and drinking milk. My American trip has certainly been full of surprises. And you are the best surprise of them all." He chuckled and gave her a milky kiss.

"Yes, all this started with the shock of my car door flying open in the parking garage, - - - - -to this." She finished the last of the milk. "I'm going to put the tray down stairs, and brush my teeth. Be back in a flash."

She just took some time to wash up the tray, and put the dishes in the dishwasher. When she snapped off the light in the upstairs hall, and walked around the bed to climb in, she found Alistair had fallen asleep. She curled up next to him, snuggled comfortably, stared up at the ceiling and smiled. It may not be hot sex with him, but being next to him was nearly as good, because she loved him, and hoped this relationship would last forever.

Sometime in the middle of the night Jenna was awakened by Alistair kissing her. "I think my arm is strong enough to allow me to make love to you."

"There are more ways to make love than 'man superior'." She sat up and slipped off her nightgown and dropped in to the floor. She began slipping off his pajama bottoms, and found him aroused and ready for anything she wanted to do.

"Jenna, *are* you quite sure- - - -?" His hands strayed to her smooth bare back and he held her close.

She straddled him, and bent down to place her mouth on his. "Just relax and enjoy." Jenna whispered in his ear and nibbled on it. 'When- - -you're stronger,- - - - - oh yes that's nice." He was exploring her back as far as he could reach. "We can- - - do *it* any which way we choose. Mmm, Oh,- - - -yes, - - - - . She took a deep breath. "This is good!"

Claire and Mac returned late Sunday evening, and found Jenna baking cookies. She turned with a smile. "How was your drive back?"

"We were forced to drive on snowy and slushy roads the first 90 miles or so. The storm has not quite made it south yet. We had some snow flurries at the higher elevations. We'll more than likely to see it here tomorrow." Mac walked over to the cookies on a cooling rack and picked up one.

Alistair came in from the den. "Glad to you two made it home." He patted Mac's back, and gave Claire a little hug.

"You two, been behaving yourselves?" Claire asked. She eyed Jenna's rosy face.

"Sure." Jenna gave Alistair a knowing smile and turned back to her cookies.

"Absolutely." Alistair grinned at Jenna. "May I sample a cookie?"

She pulled out a paper towel, and scooped up two for him.

"Can we help you gather in your luggage?" Alistair said, and followed Mac back out to the car.

Once all the luggage was inside, Mac took his milk and cookies to the table. "Okay all of you it's time for a update." They all sat down and Mac began to tell them what had transpired in London.

*****

"Rutledge arrested? That *is* a surprise. And he sent me to Utah to have the disc stolen from me, dead or alive?" Alistair said, his eyes narrowed, and he scowled.

"We now know that he told the NK's stealing the disc would be a good idea, and told them about your trip here. We think that Tina Woo may have tried to steal a copy of the disc from *Ultimate Batteries, Corp,* but could not. So, she told her co-conspirators to follow you." Mac said.

"Change of subject. Our assignment is, that you, me and the 'battery boys' in Provo, are to build a prototype combination computer with one of their batteries in something like this." Mac went to his bag and produced two small notebook size computers.

"That is going to a design challenge, because we originally wanted batteries for desk top computers, and large screen televisions." Alistair said.

"That's why you and I are going to report to their warehouse on Tuesday morning, bright and early." Mac said.

"Where are we going to stay? I was hoping I could rent a car and drive down from Jenna's condo." Alistair frowned, and touched Jenna's hand.

"Sorry Bud. You and I are going to be roommates for the next week or so. However long it takes to complete our assigned task. The feds have booked us a room at the *Hampton Inn,* just off I-15. It's only about three miles from the *Ultimate Batteries* warehouse."

"I'm going to be a temporary widow, again?" Claire's voice rose in irritation.

"Sorry Babe." Mac made an easy punch at Claire's shoulder. "Duty calls. Besides, we are going to be amply paid."

"Al, on both sides of the Atlantic, they consider you an important part of the team. The FBI doesn't want you driving our busy roads in a manner you are unaccustomed, especially in snowy weather.

When all of our experimenting is over, your acting CEO, Carruthers, wants you back in England, hale and hearty."

"I'm sorry Al. I was hoping you could come for a visit, maybe on the weekends, depending how long this task will take." Jenna said, and made a sad face and gave a little shrug.

"I have an idea. If they don't finish before the weekend, Jenna, you and I can drive to the motel and have a reunion of sorts. Unless they all decide to work straight through until all these guys come up with a satisfactory product." Claire frowned at Mac.

"We'll have to take it one day at the time. Meanwhile, Al, you and I will have to leave tomorrow midday, to check into the motel by six P.M." Mac said. "Here is your expense account." He handed Alistair a sheet from his briefcase. "Your new boss wants you to be comfortable. He said to buy some clothes if you need them, or some personal items."

Alistair glanced at the papers. "This seems quite generous. I call him tomorrow and thank him."

Claire swallowed the last of her milk. "I don't know about the rest of you, but I and my interior 'bundle' are tired." She patted her belly. "Good night, all." She picked up her overnight bag and headed for the stairs.

Mac followed his wife to bed, and Jenna began cleaning up the cookie baking pans and bowls.

Alistair moved close and embraced her. "I'm sorry, Jenna. I was looking forward to seeing your condo, and sharing it with you for a few days." He whispered into her hair, and kissed her temple.

"I know. Maybe it will take you and the others several days to complete your project. This work week has only four days. Perhaps we can be together on Friday." She wrapped her arms around him placed her mouth on his. "Let me finish up the dishes, and I'll be up soon."

He reached around her and took another cookie from the plate. "Hurry, I'll be waiting."

Eight a.m. January Third, Provo, Utah

The parking lot leading up to the *Ultimate Batteries* warehouse was deserted, but for one car. The lot had not been plowed since the last snow storm the day before. Mac and Alistair were forced to tromp through half a foot of snow, to the side door. Luckily it was open.

"Good morning." John held the door open as they entered carrying the computers and briefcases. "I've just come in and turned on the heat down here. Let's go upstairs to the office. It will warm up there more quickly." He turned to Mac. "I'm sorry, I have not met you." He put out his hand.

"I'm Dexter MacCandlass, liaison to the FBI. Call me Mac." He shook John's hand, and followed him up stairs.

"Hello everyone. I'm coming up." Paul Reacher called out.

Alistair set the two computers on the big oval table. "These are two of the smallest computers my company manufactures."

"Wow, they are small." Paul turned to John. "Let's go downstairs where the specs for our small batteries are downloaded."

Once they were all down on the main floor, Mac said. "Point me to a computer, because I have the internal designs of *Notebook #381-d* on this disc."

"Sit over here." John motioned to a computer. "This was Tina's computer. I still have a hard time believing she was emailing classified information to North Korea." He frowned, stared at the floor and put his hands in his pants pockets.

Mac shook his head. "I know, sometimes an individual's motives are hard to understand." He turned and booted up the computer, and began to download the information on the disc, and their work began.

Chapter Twenty-six

It was nearly eight that evening when Alistair and Mac climbed into Mac's car. Instead of driving straight to the motel, Mac jagged south to the nearest Walmart.

"Are we dining at the Walmart this evening?' Alistair teased.

"No, come on. We need to make a little shopping trip." Once they walked into the busy store, Mac made a beeline for the kitchen electronics area. "I can't handle another long, work day without coffee." He grumped.

*****

"You're correct. I didn't see a coffee maker anywhere in the place. No tea either, though they have a microwave. I wouldn't mind a cup of tea from time to time."

Mac selected a four-cup drip model, and then went into the grocery area and found a small bag of coffee, a box of tea and a package of cubed sugar.

Alistair picked up two lemons. "Anything else? Since we have a hot breakfast at the motel every morning, what else would you like? I know what *I* need." He roamed around the store for awhile, and finally selected packages of socks and underwear. After shopping at the Walmart, they picked up hamburgers, and went back to the motel.

They were both exhausted, and Alistair's arm and shoulder were throbbing. He decided to take a hot shower. When he came out of the bathroom, Mac was on his phone talking to Dan Forester. He said good night and hung up the phone.

"How's Dan? He's a good sort to work with." Alistair said.

"He's still assigned to the case. The Salt Lake guys seemed to have lost Tina."

"Lost her!? How could that be? I thought they were deporting her."

"It seems that the Korean consulate hired a lawyer for her. Some guy who spends his time keeping illegals in the U.S. She has a hearing at the end of the week. Where she is now, they don't know. So, we are to be vigilant if we see her. Not to approach her, just take note as to where we see her, and what car she may be driving." Mac sighed, and rubbed his green, now blood shot eyes.

"I thought the 'sticky' part of this 'caper' as you call it, was over." Alistair said.

Mac shook his head, as he pulled back the duvet on his bed. "I guess we're still all very much involved. I'd better warn Jenna."

While Mac brushed his teeth, Alistair rang Jenna's cell phone, but she did not answer, and his message went to her voice mail. He hoped she would listen to her messages tonight. He would try again in the morning. Right then he felt as tired, as Mac looked. They settled in, locked the door and turned off the lights.

*****

Jenna sat at her kitchen table picking at the hasty dinner she had fixed for herself. She was using, her kitchen as a den to work on notes for the next day at the office. She was forced to work at a kitchen table, because she had not purchased desk for her desk top computer. Her plan was to furnish an office in the smaller bedroom upstairs, and do all her work there. She'd had little time to shop for furniture since moving to Salt Lake, and she had only been in this condo for six days.

What had been she thinking when she had invited Alistair to share her condo, even for a few days?

When she moved to Salt Lake from Southern California, she'd come with little in the way of furniture. A bedroom set, a kitchen table and four chairs, and a used love seat, size sofa, and of course, her TV. Now she had another room to furnish, and she needed to shop for furniture as well as those little accessories that would reflect her tastes, like and dislikes.

Sitting at the table she studied the room with new eyes. What would Alistair think of her partially furnished place? The owners had renovated these four larger condos in order to attract buyers or long-term renters in this busy housing market. Apartments were going up all over the city. And young professionals were flocking to the new housing.

This apartment she had leased for a year was at least 25 years old. It was close to the down town area, and was less expensive than she would have to pay for a comparable a new structure. The owners had gutted the kitchen and put in new appliances. They also separated the living room from the kitchen with a long curved, black and white kitchen bar.

The picture window in the living room which had been a mainstay of living rooms in the early nineties had been replaced by three sash windows, with double pane glass side by side. They were covered with a textured cotton drape in a pleasant, warm beige tone. The fireplace on the north side of the room had been replaced with a gas burning unit. It had been updated with a small beige brick exterior, with side trim of black, along with a black hearth. The color scheme was enhanced in the solid surface counter top in the kitchen with beige, black, brown and cream specks.

She glanced at her front door, and walked the few steps to it and stroked its shiny black surface. She had fallen in 'love' with this door. Luckily, her blond oak table and chairs fit well into the color scheme.

The used sofa had a tweed pattern with beige and red predominating. It was not only sagged, it was faded. She studied her condo. Would Alistair like it? Could he live comfortably in it with her? Was it large enough to accommodate both their needs and desires? But first, would they ever have a chance to be together on it?

She went upstairs and checked the closet space. In the master bedroom there was a roomy walk-in closet. There was plenty of room for more clothes.

When she moved north and east from Southern California, she had brought her California clothes, but they were not what she needed for seven months or so of winter and early spring weather in Northern Utah.

As she stood in the doorway of the second bedroom, the phone rang. She made a dash down stairs to pick it up. "Hi?"

"Jenna, I'm glad to have reached you. I called last night, but you did not pick up."

"I'm sorry Al, I may have been the shower. How goes the work at the warehouse? Is it good to be back on a job?"

"Yes, we are still in the testing phase, but I wanted to check with you to see if you are still planning to come down Friday evening. Also, the FBI gentlemen have lost Tina Woo, and they wanted to alert everyone involved in the case. So, I suppose all I can suggest is that you be vigilant."

"Answer to question number one. Yes, I am coming down, and number two. I'll watch my back. Wasn't she supposed to be deported?"

"Yes, but she has retained an attorney, and has a hearing Friday. Hang on, Mac is knocking at the door." She heard the phone plop on something soft, the bed? Then she heard male voices. Then AL picked the phone." Hi, he has brought Dan with him, so I'd better hang up. Call you tomorrow. Loves and kisses, Bye."

"Bye?" and the line went dead. Loves and kisses, what did that mean? She hoped it meant what she wanted it to mean. She closed her eyes, and in her mind's eye she could see a large heart with the initials inside. A.P. loves J.B. Meaning: Alistair Powell loves Jenna Barlow.

*****

The next morning Mac walked over to John studying a small battery prototype under the microscope. "How did the test go?" Mac asked, as he walked over to the long plank work table. On it laid the notebook number 380-1, and John had taken the battery prototype from it, and was examining it.

"The battery stopped working sometime during the night." John Jamison answered and he bent over the project and pulled on latex gloves. "I'm going to take the battery apart."

"What about the notebook? We can examine it and find out the time it shut down." Mac stood watching John, hands on his hips.

"May I study it while you work on the battery?" Alistair said. He went to a hook on the wall holding a box of latex gloves.

"Sure, it's your product." John stalked away from the table holding the offending battery, and set it on another table. He looked up watching Alistair at his work.

Alistair glanced around the table. "It shut down at three- thirty A. M. Not bad since we booted up the notebook at four- nineteen P.M. yesterday afternoon."

"Still, it did not run for minimum of 16 hours we were hoping for." John scowled. He placed the tiny battery under the stereoscope and began examining it.

"I'm making coffee. Mac announced. "Al, you want a cup?"

"I wouldn't mind some. Thank you." Alistair answered.

"Doesn't that stuff raise your blood pressure?" John tossed a look over his shoulder.

"Possibly, perhaps a little higher than drinking a coke." Mac eyed John's open can of the beverage by his computer. Mac went on with his task.

The side door opened and a curl of fog entered with him. "Morning guys. How did the test go?" Paul Reacher turned and slammed the door shut.

John looked up at his friend with a deep frown. "The battery didn't make it the 16 hours. We need to rework it."

"I'll be with you in a minute." He walked to the coat tree near the table where snacks were sometimes found, and Mac was pouring coffee. Next to that table was a fridge, and he shoved a sack in it.

"Your wife made you a lunch this morning?" John said with an edge in his voice.

"Yes, she didn't have to work today, so she had time." Paul glanced at his friend with a slight smile and a toss of his head. "Now, let me take a look at that battery."

The lab became a busy workplace, full of tension as the four men focused on improving their products, and the work day progressed.

*****

Friday afternoon Alistair called Jenna. "Hi Al, What's up?" She said as she recognized his cell phone number before clicking on.

"Mac has gone to attend a meeting with a state agency chief. They need to finalize the test we're planning to conduct in the desert west of the capital city. I must ask you for a ride to the motel, because we will be meeting Clair and Mac, and then go to supper."

"You want me to come pick you up from the warehouse?" She laughed.

"Yes, I won't be finished with my work here, until around six P.M. Do you need directions?"

"Yes, that would help. If the fog is as thick there, as it is in here in our capital city."

"You have fog, too? I thought it was heavy here, because we're so close to Utah Lake. It reminds me of my home, and just as cold. Oh yes, directions." He cleared his throat. "Take the second Provo exit from the carriage, excuse me, Freeway. Turn west for about three miles, and then take a road called Fifth West, strange name for a road." He mumbled. "Drive south, and you'll see two warehouses. We're in the more southern one."

"Thank you for the directions. We have here, in Northern Utah, what is called a temperature inversion. It happens when we have snow on the ground. A cold high pressure comes in and presses on the warmer, moist air trapping it in lower places. It's cold, toxic, just plain icky. Welcome to Utah fog. Or what they call a Wasatch Front Inversion."

"Thank you for the weather update." He chuckled

"I'll leave the office around five P.M. I should get there a little after six. Before you leave the relative warmth of the warehouse, listen for my car. If you stand outside for very long, you'll turn into a Popsicle. See ya." She clicked off.

Chapter Twenty-Seven

Alistair was tidying up, when he heard a car pull up close to the warehouse door. Everyone else had left, because it *was* a Friday, and the four of them had managed to solve the battery problem, and even lengthen the battery's life. A notebook and its new battery were ready to test. That is if the FBI could manage to find a site everyone agreed on. Especially since the plan was to use the small computer as a trigger hooked to explosives.

He picked up his coat, and searched his pockets for gloves. This weather was more and more reminding him of London. In most winters his home city was gripped in the winter fog and freezing rain.

In his left hand he had the key to the door, and his briefcase was tucked under his right arm. Now he stepped out, and locked the door. The only light came from safety lights high on the roof of the building, and that light seemed to flicker and wave through the fog.

The car parked ten feet or so from the door was dark, not Jenna's silver Lexus. He hesitated, because a warning bell went off in his head. He stared into the soupy air and could not see any other car coming down the side road.

A figure darted out from behind the dark car, and yelled at him. "Alistair Powell, I'm going to kill you!"

"What, who are you? What are you saying?" He yelled, and backed closer to the door, he had just locked.

"You've ruined my life. You should have died, when Chin shot you. But no, you had the luck of jumping into an unlocked car, and that Barlow bitch saved you. You both need to die." She waved a pistol in his direction.

Alistair's hands shook, but he tapped down his fear, and forced himself to stand tall, and speak in a soft voice. "Was the disc that important to you, Tina?" He asked.

"Yes, you're so stupid. That's why I was sent here. My country needs the technology that is being invented, and refined here. Our officials knew how easy it was to get into America, especially to dupe the local University. They welcome foreign students. They think we'll convert to their religion."

"Perhaps after this experience with you, they'll become a little more selective." He spoke as calmly as he could.

"I doubt it. If some other student- - -, well that's their problem not mine anymore. They want to love everybody, Ha!" She took a step closer, and he moved a tiny step toward to the left side of her car.

He suddenly realized that she first needed to vent her anger. Perhaps if he could just keep her talking, especially the way she waved that weapon back and forth. She didn't seem too familiar with it.

Faintly he heard another car's engine coming toward them. He hoped it wasn't Jenna.

Jenna turned her car down the lane that led to the warehouse. The fog was as thick as, not pea soup, but much like the beach at night, during the winter in Southern California.

Under the lights of the warehouse, she could see Alistair standing, gesturing at someone. She felt an alarm of fear, but along with that a sense of heightened tension. She turned off the headlights, and angled her car close to the first warehouse, and cut the engine. She zipped her up her coat, and pulled up the hood over her blonde hair, now Jenna managed to see the other figure, smallish, wearing a dark parka. Something glinted in the left hand. Was that a weapon of some kind? Possibly a gun? Jenna exited her car and softly shut the door. Pressing her body against the warehouse, she moved slowly toward the individual waving a gun. Once she cleared the warehouse wall, she would be seen by Alistair, but hopefully not the individual who was holding the weapon aimed at him.

She watched the hood of the dark coat, as it slipped down. Jenna could the see the figure directly ahead. With the hood down she could see long black hair. Tina! Jenna smiled. *I'm at least three inches taller and weigh at least ten pounds more than her.* She glanced down at her own boots. She could run up behind the girl and knock her down, but in order to do that successfully, she must inch closer.

Alistair glanced in Jenna's direction, but showed no sign that he saw her. He kept asking Tina questions. He was trying to keep the girl's focus on him.

The ground was wet and beginning to freeze over. There were piles of old snow along the edge of the warehouse. Jenna carefully stepped out and began to creep toward the screaming girl.

*****

"Now I'm going to be deported, and because of you, I've lost my scholarship at the university. They won't let me register for winter semester courses, and they've even kicked me out of my dormitory rom. You deserve to die Alistair Powell, you've ruined my life."

"If you kill me, Tina, they'll arrest you, and you'll be convicted, and you might even get the death penalty. I believe Utah has that law on the books." He continued to edge toward Tina's car.

"No, now I don't care. My life is over. I'll go home in disgrace. Here I had a good life. And John Jamison liked me. We had something going on between us." Tears ran down her face, and she pushed her hair away from her cheeks.

At that moment Jenna wound the long strap of her shoulder bag, gripped it in her left hand and ran at Tina aiming the bag at the girl's head. The blow dropped Tina to her knees, and the gun skittered out of her hand. As it slid across the icy blacktop, Jenna threw her whole weight at Tina's back and flattened her to the ground. Jenna knew that move. She had learned it from the boys in her family when she was a child. She dropped both her knees on Tina's shoulders and pushed hard. The girl tried to twist her body under Jenna to throw her off, but Jenna had weight and strength, that the smaller girl lacked. She watched in relief as Alistair ran for the gun, found it and scooped it up.

"Al, go to my car." Jena yelled. "Under the front seat is a roll of duct tape. Please get it." Jenna asked. The girl squirmed under her, but Jenna she slammed Tina's face unto the cold blacktop's surface. "Threaten my boy friend, will you. You're dead meat!"

Alistair returned with the tape and was tearing a long piece, when he reached the two women on the ground. Jenna let up enough on Tina's shoulders, so could Alistair pull the girl's arms behind her back and tape her wrists together.

"Let me go! You'll be sorry. There are others of my people. They will come after you, destroy you." Tina screamed.

"Shut up bitch, or I'll tape your mouth." Jenna yelled down at the girl.

Alistair unceremoniously dragged Tina up and set her down by the side of the warehouse. He already had his cell phone out and punched in Mac's number. He listened to his friend for a few seconds, and then called 911. He glanced over at Jenna. "Mac is on his way, as well as the police."

Jenna stood up and took stock of her clothes. She found a hole ripped over her left knee. She had torn her brand-new tan corduroy pants. "Ugh. All this nasty behavior on your part Tina has cost me a pair of slacks. Why did you come here in the first place?"

Jenna stomped over to Tina and gazed down at her. "What were you thinking? Now you've made your situation even worse for your future." The girl was now weeping uncontrollably. Jenna gave her a look of disgust and turned away.

Alistair came and put an arm around his lady. "Did you really mean it when you said 'my boyfriend'?" He grinned.

"Yes, I consider you, my boyfriend; Even though we've only known each other for less than two weeks." She laughed. "It seems like so much longer."

The sound of sirens brought their heads up and they watched through the heavy cold fog for the police car. The police were quick to put Tina in the patrol car. "The first officer smiled. "Duct tape, huh? Do you carry that around with you just in case you have to restrain someone?" His eyes crinkled in to a smile.

"It comes in handy for many situations." Jenna said. "Do you want us to follow you to your offices to make a statement?"

The policeman nodded. "Yes ma'am."

Mac and Claire came next and the four of them followed the squad car back to police headquarters housed in the Utah County Court Building.

Mac climbed out of the car and put a hand on Alistair's shoulder. "I leave you alone for three hours and you manage to have someone come by and try to kill you. I'm going to put you on a leash." He rolled his eyes.

*****

When Alistair and Jenna walked out of the police headquarters section, it was nearly nine p.m. Claire called and invited them back to the motel for a supper of sorts. "Mac went for a pizza and a salad, while I found us some dessert."

Jenna was yawning by the time she sampled a cookie: Claire's version of dessert. "I'm sorry; it's been an eventful day."

"It seems the four of us have had an eventful two weeks. Claire said. "Come on Mac, my love. Let us go to the room I booked."

"No need for you two to move. Jenna and I can take the extra room." Alistair said.

"No, the room I booked has a king-sized bed. We'll let you two flip a coin to see who sleeps in which queen-sized bed." She winked at Alistair, and began gathering up her coat and overnight bag. Mac followed her with his belongings.

"We'll see you two tomorrow, not too early. Good night." Mac closed the door.

Jenna collapsed on the nearest bed. "Oh, this is a comfortable bed. Mac chose this motel well." She sat up and kicked off her boots, but dragged her body off the bed and set the boots in the closet.

"While you get comfortable, I'm going to take a shower." Alistair hurried to the bathroom. Later, when he came out, he found Jenna had undressed, donned her nightshirt, and curled up in the bed facing the wall. He stood over her, and found she was quite asleep. Her hands tucked near her head, like a little girl. He yawned and blinked, and found he was tired, too. Snapping off the lights, and turning down the thermostat on the heater under the window, he stood and gazed out into the foggy night. All in all, he felt quite lucky for still being alive. And even better and thankful for having met Jenna. Best of all, because he now had Jenna in his life, and hopefully into the future. He prayed that this New Year would bring a promise of them being together always.

Now if he and Jenna could only work out their lives, so that they *could* be together. That could make his life so much better, and he would be a truly happy man. He would think on that, and talk to her tomorrow.

CHAPTER TWENTY-EIGHT

The four of them had an easy, yet enjoyable weekend. While the girls went shopping, Mac and Alistair watched a college basketball game on TV. To Alistair, this game was much easier to understand than football. The goal was to make a basket, or to keep the opposing team from doing so. He could understand why the players were tall, most of them African-Americans. These were college teams from leagues all over America playing against each other.

When the girls returned, they dumped their purchases on the big bed and began sorting through them. "Look at this!" Jenna held up a tiny white dress with little rosebuds sewed on the bodice. "I couldn't resist it."

Mac looked over. "Did you decide we're having a girl, Claire?"

"I didn't, but the ultrasound did." She laughed.

"Thanks for telling me." He grumped.

"I would have last night, but we became otherwise involved." She tilted her head, and flashed him a wide-eyed smile.

"Okay, I forgive you." His lips twitched. "But let me ask you this. Isn't that little dress a bit impractical? I thought we would dress the baby in overalls, and tee shirts for the first year of so."

"Well yes, but every girl needs a dress to look pretty in, even if she's only three months old." Claire went back to sorting through the sacks and boxes. One held a pair of tiny patent leather shoes.

*****

On Sunday, to get out of the fog, they drove up into the mountains: Destination: a ski resort called *Sundance*. "Why is this resort called Sundance? It should be called Snow Dance, or something more appropriate." Alistair asked with a jovial air.

"The resort is owned by the actor Robert Redford. Supposedly he named it after the most notable character he has ever portrayed in film." Jenna said.

"You're referring to: *Butch Cassidy and the Sundance Kid?*" Alistair asked. "I saw that film many years ago. I remember some of his others that I have enjoyed. Sundance, eh? It does have a name one would remember."

They went into the cafeteria and could watch skiers gliding down the hill through its huge windows. Then they went through the cafeteria lime for lunch, and watched the skiers while eating for a while longer. "I can see the attraction of being up here, especially when the valley is covered in fog. It's amazing; the sky is so clear and so blue. Do any of you ski?' Alistair asked.

"I do." Claire said. "I learned as a teenager."

"I took it up last fall. There's a small ski resort fairly close to St. George." Mac said.

"I thought about learning the sport, when I knew I was being transferred to Salt Lake."Jenna said.

"It looks exhilarating and fun." Alistair mused. "Perhaps someday I could have a chance to give a go at it."

"I think we'd better go back to the motel. The women have to drive back to their places of employment, and we have to be up, and ready to drive to the west desert early tomorrow." Mac said.

Monday, January 8th, High Desert, west of Salt Lake City

Two large vans pulled off the highway, drove south and bumped across the winter clad desert to a wash picked out from a satellite scan. Every twig and stunted bush that covered surface of the desert floor was coated with a glittering combination of snow and frost. It looked like a Disney- created Fairyland. The sun, low in the south-eastern sky, gave off a cold, golden light. Its glow wavered through the dense fog.

Nine men climbed out of the vans. Some carried certain equipment, and two were dressed in heavily padded suits. They were from the FBI bomb squad. Alistair and Paul Reacher carefully set the plastic covered notebook in a shielded spot in the dry wash. The bomb squad carried explosives in a wooden box, and in a matter of minutes they had the bomb in the box hooked up to the notebook sized computer. They noted the time set, and booted up the small notebook.

Two other men set up a camera on the closest power pole. Mac rubbed his gloved hands together, and pulled down his English woolen cap over his ears. Even though there was no wind, it was bone chillingly cold. With each breath the men took, moisture came out of their throats in streams of white. He touched his nose with his gloved hand, and wondered if was still resting there, a frozen lump on his face.

Paul turned to the computer, and opened it to the program it was to carry out. Carefully, he hooked the lines of wires across the wash, to the bomb squad and their sets of fuses. They hooked the wires to the box holding the explosives. When all was in place, Director Carlson waved them all back to the vehicles. "Since we're all out here freezing off our butts, I scheduled for a breakfast at the *Cracker Barrel Restaurant*. Follow me." They drove back in the direction of the Salt Lake Valley.

After breakfast Mac, Alistair, John and Paul returned to the warehouse in Provo. Alistair and Mac began to finish up their work on the computers and file it. Alistair, stood and began to pace in restless circles. "I wish there was a gymnasium nearby. I need a jog."

Mac glanced at him. "Your shoulder must be feeling better. It's tough to be here in the winter. If you don't ski or snowshoe, you're stuck indoors for a workout."

"It's the same way in England. "We're about finished here, aren't we? If the notebook performs as planned, that will mean that I must return home to the UK; Most likely, no later than Wednesday. With Carruthers now in command of the home office, I'm needed at the factory."

Mac stood and began to pace around with Alistair. They moved to a corner of the warehouse. "I understand, buddy. You've had quite the 'ride' here in the States. The best part of the adventure I'm sure, was meeting Jenna."

Alistair stopped and dug the toe of his boot into a tiny crack in the concrete floor. "Yes, I've come to the conclusion that I love her. I could take her to England with me, but the life she would give up here is better than one than I could provide for her in the UK." He ran his hand through his thick, dark brown, hair.

"Talk to her. She may see the relationship differently that you do." Mac returned to his computer.

At four- thirty A.M. the next morning the land line in Mac and Alistair's motel room rang. Mac groped for the phone and in a foggy voice answered. "Yes?"

"The notebook performed without a hitch. We have a 'nice', thorough explosion on tape. It fed into our hook-up about ten minutes ago." Director Carlson sounded almost gleeful. "We're calling everyone involved into our offices at about eleven-thirty this morning for a debriefing. So, get a few hours sleep and we'll see you later late morning."

Alistair sat up in bed. "Was that call about the explosion?"

"Yeah, that was Carlson. He could have waited until a decent hour." Mac stood and stretched. "We're supposed to all meet in Salt Lake at eleven- thirty A.M. "If you can, go back to sleep."

"Good idea." Alistair said, as he located his cell phone, and went into the bathroom to call Carruthers. When he finished his call, he climbed back into bed, but lay there for a long, long time. His mind drifted back to meeting Jenna, her kindness and care of his gunshot wound. How efficient, and how pretty she is and is such a good cook. He couldn't lose her. But how could he work out his life to be able to return here to this especially interesting area of America? He knew he must go home to 'put his life in order'. But he would return here, he *had* to.

*****

When Mac and Alistair arrived, most of the team that had been in the desert the early morning before, were already there. Dan Forester from the Las Vegas office joined them. On a side table in the board room, sat a variety of box lunches, a bucket of chilled sodas and a coffee pot.

Director Carlson greeted them. "We'll begin this meeting with the video of the explosion." A large retractable screen was in place at one end of the long room. A video player was connected to it.

In the darkened room they watched 44 seconds of the explosion, one in real time and once again in slow motion. Next, the picture cut to the remains of the bomb, and the computer box. Only bits and pieces of both remained. The detonation was thorough and complete. Carlson had the tech shut off the video and turned up the lights in the room.

"As you can see the explosion was triggered at four forty- three A.M. It was a clean explosion, and the notebook-battery combination worked flawlessly."

CHAPTER TWENTY-NINE

Harper, one of the bomb experts spoke up. "From the evidence, I'd stake my expertise, that a small computer like this one could definitely be used to trigger a much larger explosive device; Possibly, even one with field nuclear capability. The remote control, with a timing devise of 16 hours would give the initiators of the bomb explosion amazing flexibility. This triggering device would be sought after by several groups hostile to the United States as well as other western countries." He turned to Carlson.

"I'm afraid the four of you, Reacher, Jamison, MacCandlass, and Powell, have opened a Pandora's Box." There was a heavy silence in the room, and everyone looked around at each member of the group. "I'm recommending that the notebook 380-I and the specific battery built for it will go under classified information. All specifications for the building of this mechanism will receive highest National Security clearance."

"So, our technology will be buried." John Jamison scowled and shifted in his chair.

"That's correct. You are free to go ahead and work on the larger units with World Wide Limited." Carlson said.

"Listen John, we have several projects lined up with World Wide. We have months of work to keep us busy." Paul Reacher said.

"I know, but it's just one more example of the government interfering with our lives." John groused.

Carlson managed to keep his facial expression passive, as he passed around a set of documents to each one of the men present. "These are to be signed by each one of you. You must not disclose any of what has been seen or discussed here today. It's now a matter of national security."

Mac nodded and grabbed his document and signed it, as did Dan

Forester. Alistair read it over carefully and signed it, too. Suddenly he was struck with the vital necessity that this technology be buried.

John studied the papers, frowned and watched everyone else sign there's. "Is this really necessary?"

Mac stood and walked over to John and put a firm hand on his shoulder. "Let it go. What we did is now out of our hands. Sign the damn paper." He watched as John signed his name in a bold signature.

*****

Now Alistair was ready to call Jenna, he had booked a flight home to England and was packed and nearly ready to depart. "Jenna, hi pretty lady. How are you this Tuesday evening?"

"Alistair, how did the test go?"

"It went off without any errors. So, now I am needed back in the factory. I must return to England."

"You're leaving tomorrow, aren't you?" There was a hitch in her voice.

"Yes, my flight leaves at two- twenty P.M. on Delta. Mac just called Claire, and he will take me to the terminal and then make straightway back to Rawley."

"I wish you didn't have to go. I was hoping for another weekend with you." She sniffed, and became silent for a beat. He could hear her, as she cleared her throat.

He jumped into the conversation. "I'm sorry I must leave, too. We both knew I would, Jenna. I love you. My dream would be that we could be together, forever." He exhaled a large breath.

"I believe, yes I know I love you too. And if you like, I'd be pleased to marry you. I'm not sure how we're going to work through this seven thousand mile distance situation, but I'm willing to give it a try."

"You'd marry me?!"

"Didn't I just say that?" A shaky laugh came out.

"Would you have a child with me? I think I'd like to be a father." He said in a soft voice.

"Of course! What a strange request? That's what marriage is all about. Loving and having a family to love, too."

"Jenna, love. I'm going to find a way to get back to you, and be with you. Please, pray for us. Once you were in a religious organization; you certainly learned how to pray correctly. Do that for us. And I'll try too. I must go now. I'll call you when I arrive in Newark." I must say goodbye for now."

*****

She was waiting on a bench in the air terminal directly behind the Delta check-in. She jumped up and stood in line with him while he checked in at the front desk. They walked together until he was forced to go through security.

He threw his arms around her and kissed her soundly. "Wait for me, Jenna. I'll return to you, because we must be together." He kissed her forehead, and gave her one last hug.

Her last glimpse of him was as he stepped in for a security check.

She watched until he was swallowed up into the crowd of travelers. She had knowledge in her head and her heart, that he would return, and they would someday be together.

*****

Jenna opened the rear door of her condo. She glanced at the storage closet in the utility room. She smiled at her nearly new skis stored in the closet. She pulled out a hanger from the closet and admired her new ski parka. She stroked the sleeve, and felt the silky, padded black fabric. The front of the jacket boasted a jaunty slash of white and light green fabric, a fashionable contrast against the black fabric.

Upstairs in her bedroom closet hung the rest of the outfit. She would wear each piece of it on her ski outing tomorrow. This would be her third day on the slopes, and she could hardly wait. Yet, she really wished that Alistair could to be with her, so they could learn this fascinating new activity together.

She walked the few paces to her kitchen area and tossed her coat on the sofa. Opening the fridge door, she and began a search for something to eat for supper.

After changing into soft, worn jeans and a sweat shirt, she ate her simple fare while scanning the TV Guide. Perhaps she would find some program to catch and hold her attention this Friday evening. It was February 24th, and the last time she had talked to Alistair had been ten days before, when he called to wish her a Happy Valentine's Day. The next day a box of expensive English teas and chocolates had arrived in the mail. She had mailed him a humorous thank you card.

After watching TV for most of the evening, she grew sleepy, and turned it off. She must be up and ready by eight- thirty A.M. when her friend Sara came to pick her up. Jenna went upstairs to bed and soon fell asleep. She had been in bed about half an hour when the phone rang. *That must be Sara reminding me to be ready early tomorrow.*

"Hello?' She sat upright in her bed when she heard Alistair's voice. It set a delicious shock wave through her. "Al, how are you?" She glanced at the clock: eleven- twenty P.M. "You're up early?" She laughed nervously.

"Yes, a little past five A.M. I believe. And, of course still dark out, and raining. What I called to ask about, what are your plans for tomorrow?"

"Tomorrow? I'm going skiing. I took lessons, and I'm really enjoying it. Tomorrow will be the third time I can go up to the ski resort and my last lesson, I hope. It's a wonderful place to be, especially on a sunny day." Jenna answered.

"Do you think you could come pick me up at Salt Lake International? Say about seven P.M. tomorrow evening?" There was laughter, yet hope in his voice.

"You're coming here?!" She squealed. Her breath seemed to leave her body.

"Yes, for a fairly long period. I'm going to work with the young men in Provo for several weeks." He sounded a little breathless, too.

"Of course, I'll come fetch you. Oh Al, I'm having a hard time believing that I will see you in about 20 hours." She said with a shaky laugh.

"A request. Would you wear your skiing clothing? I want to see you in that outfit."

"I will, I promise. Until tomorrow then, I love you." She wished she could climb through the land line right into his arms.

"Love you. Good bye." He clicked off.

As she set the phone back into its cradle she glanced around the room. *Clean sheets, fresh towels, I must get to work.* For the next half hour she cleaned, straightened. Put linens in the washer. Everything must be fresh.

As she finally slid into her fresh, clean bed, she had delicious thoughts of her precious Alistair, here with her. She was grateful, that she had bought some furnishings for this place, found some little additions to her decorating scheme. Finally, she closed her eyes, and willed herself to sleep. A trick she had taught her body to do. It had been necessary when she lived in the group home. It was a way to find some inner peace and privacy, in a sometimes-chaotic atmosphere.

Chapter Thirty

Alistair sat waiting in the pick-up area wrapped in a great coat, and hat. She stopped the car, jumped out and ran around to lift the back hatch. Once he hefted in his sizeable suitcase and suit bag, he turned and pulled her up in a tight embrace and gave her a hard, quick kiss. "Drive home, woman." He laughed and squeezed her shoulder.

Once they were on the freeway, she turned to him and grabbed his hand. "How did you manage this trip? How long can you stay?"

"Well, my superior, and a few others are planning to air freight a number of televisions and desk top computers to *Ultimate Batteries Corp.* I'm going to help them assemble their products into ours. Once we have developed the specs for each specific unit, we can patent the composite in both the States and the UK. This is to safeguard our products from a group of imitators, at least for the life of the patents."

"That should take awhile? Shouldn't it?' She asked hopefully.

"I have a working visa for 90 days, and the state department sent me a letter saying that I may renew the visa if necessary." He stroked her shoulder.

They reached her condo, and she drove up the small incline to a row of garages behind the four-plex. "When they remodeled and updated these condos it was too difficult to build garages underneath. So, they built these up behind the housing. We also have some extra parking."

"Interesting, the garages are built right into the hillside. I've seen structures like this in England." He commented.

"We'll just roll your luggage across this blacktop to my back door." She hurried to the door and pulled a set of keys from her purse. She led him into a walk-through laundry room with a large storage closet on the opposite side of the washer and dryer. Next, they walked into a short hallway, and the first door on the right was a half-bath. He followed her into the living area.

The living room and kitchen flowed together. Different from Claire's house and even the cottage they stayed in at Christmas time. "You have a fireplace!"

"Yes, but it's natural gas. Saves on pollution, especially when we're have the temperature inversions in the winter." She walked to the wall and flipped two switches which lighted the gas jets. "I'll be back." She walked out to the utility closet and hung up her parka. She walked to the kitchen. "How about some dinner?"

"Absolutely." He began studying her pictures on the wall in the living room area. He stopped and stood gazing out into the night through the front window. "What a marvelous view. Being up on this hill certainly has its advantages."

"It's better upstairs in the bedroom. Go take a look." She glanced at the stair way in the small hallway near the front door.

"I think I will." He picked up his oversized valise and thumped up the stairs with it.

She smiled at his vanishing figure, but went back to her dinner preparations. Soon she had their supper ready. "Come eat." She yelled up the stairs.

They sat down at her small table, and ate a quick chicken-vegetable and salad meal. He sat back and smiled. "I'm tired, and full of good food, but I right now want you to come and sit on your pretty sofa with me."

She glanced back at the food still sitting on the kitchen bar. She wanted to jump up and immediately and put everything away, clean up the kitchen. But having Alistair here was special. She sat down next to him.

"I know enough about you, and I understand how you are somehow programmed to clean up before sitting down and doing some relaxing. Just now I feel impelled to tell you how much I care about you and that I love you." He picked up her hand. "Even though I've been married, before and I thought I understood about loving a woman. My depth of feeling for you transcends anything else I've ever known." He kissed her temple.

"Dear Alistair- - - - -, I do love- - - -."

"There's more. I'm not going to be able to live here with you. I'm scheduled to move to Provo tomorrow evening. There is another technician coming in from London on Monday. Paul Reacher has found an apartment for us. It's much cheaper than living in a motel. We will be living there for at least three months." He pulled her close and stroked the fingers on her left hand.

"Right now, most of the girls in England want a sapphire/ diamond ring like Princess Megan was given. But I think, this ring will suit you better." He handed her a ruby colored, velvet box. "This is a yellow diamond. You're such a sunny, beautiful blonde, and I picked this for you." He slid a ring with a pale-yellow stone on her finger.

She turned and planted a kiss on his mouth. "My, it's beautiful." She lifted her hand to pick up the light shining down from the kitchen ceiling. "I've never had anything so beautiful, so special."

"Do you think you could be ready for us to marry, say the end of May?" He gazed into her eyes.

"I could do that. Do you want to marry here or in England?" She asked.

"Here, first of all, and then we can go to York. There you will then become a certified English bride. Can you plan for a long vacation?'

She sat forward for a moment, and turned to him with a slight frown. "I think so. Do you plan for us to live somewhere close to your work? We can talk through the details. Anything, anywhere, so we can be together, Will we see each other every day, or must I be a single wife? I must be yours alone."

"You'll be my only wife. I have no inclination to be a polygamist." He laughed and hugged her. Then he stroked her hair away from her face, and began to kiss her again, and yet again.

Alistair sat back and laughed. "Be patient with me Jenna. I just want to hold and love you for a while. Then I'll give you time to clean up the kitchen. After that I plan to keep you busy for the whole night. And when we can marry, for the rest of our lives."

EPILOGUE

"Stop fussing or I'll never be able to put this circlet of flowers on your hair. It will end up falling into your eyes." Claire grumped. "We've only 20 minutes before Pastor Phillips expects the groom *and* the bride to be out in the chapel."

"I'm trying. Getting married is just so- - - -- - - -? I never expected the simple plan of getting married would be so stressful. That there would be so much planning, especially since we're flying out tomorrow for London." Jenna said.

"And then in these past two weeks, everyone at my job wanted to throw showers and parties for me. It was fun, but again time consuming and added more stress."

"You can relax when you get to England. Come on. Here, slide into your shoes. Okay. Now, let's take a look in the valet mirror. Oh yes, this dress is perfect. Where did you find it?" Claire asked.

"I went dress shopping, and everything I tried on or even looked at was so frilly, and expensive. So, I sketched this one, but I wanted it to be short. You know, calf length and with the thin straps rather than strapless." Jenna adjusted the gown and put out an arm for the lace shrug.

Claire slid it on her friend. "Where did you find this cotton lace shrug? It's gorgeous."

"I found it in a catalog, and bought it first. Then I went in search for a dressmaker. She found the cotton brocade fabric for the dress."

"Well, who would have thought a cotton wedding dress would turn out to be so beautiful. Now turn around. Perfect. I'll go fetch your bouquet." Claire stepped out of the small dressing room. Hurrying back, she handed the daisy bouquet to Jenna. "You really make a beautiful summer bride. Let's go." Clair walked behind Jenna, and eased her down the hall to the chapel door.

Alistair stood at the front of the rectory, tall and handsome in a dark suit and red striped tie. He was adjusting the cuffs on his shirt, most likely *not* the first time.

For Claire, however, there was a little the thrill when Mac caught her eye. He still could make her heart jump in her chest. He managed to clean up so well. He also wore a dark suit, but this time with a green silk tie, bringing out the emerald in his eyes, and burnished copper of his hair.

The few guests invited were sitting in the front pews, and Suzanne had the chore of keeping Claire and Mac's infant daughter calm and happy. Suzanne's seven-year-old son, Andrew Junior helped by waving a toy at the little girl. Being seven weeks old, baby Erin had not yet developed the skill to hang on to a rattle or toy. Yet she was dressed properly for the wedding in her dress of white purchased by her 'auntie' Jenna.

Andy, Suzanne's husband just now hustled into the rectory and sat down by his wife. The pastor took his place in front of the group. He cleared his throat. "I believe we are ready to begin." He motioned to Jenna and Claire, and they walked in. Jenna took her place next to Alistair, and Claire next to the bride.

The service began with a short talk by the Pastor concerning the sanctity of marriage. After a few moments, baby Erin began yawn and fuss. The wedding was scheduled at two p.m. and it was baby Erin's nap time, after all. Claire eyed her child. She watched until Suzanne's jiggling was not soothing the unhappy infant. Claire walked down, picked up her baby and went to the rear of the rectory, near the heavy doors. She found a pacifier in her pocket of her beige suit jacket, and eased out the door into the bright afternoon sun. It was an early summer day in St. George which meant it would be close to 90 degrees.

She found a shady spot under a spreading tree, and soothed and rocked the little girl until the crying stopped and the baby's eyes closed.

Claire's attention turned to large, older suburban as it pulled up next to the curb. A slim, young woman climbed out. She was wearing a prairie dress commonly worn by FLDS women. The dress was denim blue, and the woman was blonde, and her hair styled in a long braid down her back. Claire walked closer, and suddenly knew who the woman was. She was familiar: a younger, thinner, sadder version of the vibrant, pretty bride inside.

Claire walked over to her. "You're Jenna's sister, aren't you?" Claire asked.

The young woman looked up from the ground and nodded. "I heard a rumor that Jenna was marrying an illegal man from England and moving there. My sister wives were kind enough to drop me off here, while they shop at Costco. I just wanted to see- - - -, you know, from a distance."

"Come in." Claire took her arm. "She'll want to see you." They walked into the cool, dim room, and waited until they could see to find a seat.

Soon Pastor Phillips said. "I now pronounce you man and wife. You may kiss the bride." Alistair bent to give Jenna a small kiss.

Jenna turned to the group, and her face glowed in a radiant smile. The small audience applauded. Immediately Suzanne rushed over and gave her a hug, then turned to introduce Andrew and Andy.

Claire grabbed the FLDS sister's arm, with one hand and tucked the baby in the other arm. "We're going up to talk to her. What's your name? I'm Claire MacCandlass."

"She's so beautiful! But I can't stay, because they'll be back for me soon."

Jenna glanced up. The smile faded from her face and the shock of recognition replaced it. Claire continued to propel the FLDS girl down the side of the room until they reached the bride and groom. "Jasmine?!" Jenna shoved her bouquet into Alistair's hands and threw her arms around her sister. "It's so good to see you. I've worried and wondered,- - - - -. Are you alright? Are you happy?"

The buzz of conversation in the room stopped. All eyes were trained on the sisters' reunion. "I'm married to Heber Jensen, and have three children. The oldest is ten. You are so beautiful. and you have such a lovely dress. Did it cost lots of money? You seem to have made a good life for yourself. Did you go to college?"

"Yes, and yes. This is Alistair Powell, my- - - - - - -husband." She touched his shoulder and Jenna found her smile. It lit up her face. How has it been for you?"

The girl stopped. "It's not been easy since the Prophet's- - - -left us. We've heard rumors, I mean, that he's in prison- - - -- - - - -?"

Alistair picked up Jasmine's hand. "Such a pleasure to meet you, Jasmine. We're so happy you could come to the wedding." He smiled down at her.

She blushed. "My goodness, I love the way he talks." She turned to Jenna. "You're so lucky to meet him, and he's handsome, too."

"No, my luck was in meeting Jenna." Alistair said. The rear door swung open, and another woman wearing the same type of dress Jasmine wore, peaked in.

Jasmine pulled her hand away from Alistair's grip. "I have to go. I'm glad I saw you. Both of you." She glanced nervously at the door and moved toward it.

Pastor Phillips caught up with her and touched her arm. "Young woman, remember this church. If you ever need help, we're here to offer you refuge. You and your children." He walked to the door and held it open for her.

There was a long heavy silence in the room. Finally, Mac stood up in the front, and cleared his throat. "Lunch is served at our house. Follow me." He waved them along.

Alistair took Jenna's arm and led her out into the sunny, warm afternoon. "I'm so happy you could finally make contact with your sister. And I'm sure seeing you and *me*, were of vital importance to her, too."

"Especially today. It has made this day even more memorable." Jenna blinked away tears, and leaned against her new husband.

*****

"Mac tells me that you two are leaving for London tomorrow." Dan Forester said, as he sat near Alistair in Mac and Claire's living room.

"That's correct. We're going back to England. To York first, so that my parents, sister and brother -in-law can meet Jenna. After a few days there, we'll settle in my flat while I go back to work for a few weeks. I wanted Jenna to experience an English summer."

"Do you know how long you'll be there?" Angela Patton asked.

"Probably, three months. We want to come back around autumn. My company has some plans to expand into America, especially Utah. We've found an excellent work environment here. Jenna wants to go back to work, and we have plans to return to the Cottages where we first grew to care for each other. We're sentimental about that place."

"I think that's very romantic." Angela said wistfully.

"Even though we were first together there at Christmas time. We think this experience in the autumn will be nearly as memorable as it was last Christmas." Jenna said as she linked her arm through Alistair's.

"Though not as cold." Alistair laughed, and lightly kissed his bride.

"We wish you the best. Come on, Dan. I need to get home to my husband and son, and you have a poker game tonight, right?" Angela said.

Dan nodded. "Yeah, I need to win tonight." He stood and strolled over to Mac. "Thanks for lunch, but we must get back to Vegas, and whatever work Strickland has for us tomorrow."

"Dan, you need a wife to go home to, not a poker game." Mac touched his shoulder.

"You guys marry, and you can't stand to see anyone left single. I'm doing fine." Dan grumped.

"I'm just saying; don't knock it until you try it." Mac laughed.

"It would take a special gal to tear me away from Friday night poker."

He laughed, but to Claire his words sounded a little sad and tired.

"You'll trip over some woman, some time. Make sure you pick her up not step over her." Claire took his arm and kissed him on the cheek. "Bye Dan, Angela. Drive safe. Tomorrow is another day, and could possibly be another adventure for us all."

The End

If you would like to know why Dan Forester is no
interested in poker games, read:
BANK HEIST IN ST. GEORGE series three.

I dedicate this story to my daughter, Jenelle Hiatt
She was with me when we had the chance to go
Into the FLDS community. During that time many
of their secrets were revealed.